I *pronounce you man and wife.*"

It was over. He kissed his bride, happier than he had ever been in his life. The family went wild, hugging and kissing each other, laughing as they emerged into the sunshine.

Something must have happened, he thought, as they started down the steps. Such a big crowd, television cameras and everything.

Before he had a chance to take it in, to wonder, he felt the flash of a photographer's bulb, and a microphone was thrust into his face.

"Mr. Costello, how does it feel to be married to an heiress?"

Eva Rutland began writing when her four children, now all successful professionals, were growing up. Eva lives in California with her husband, Bill, who actively supports and encourages her writing career.

Some people marry for true love, some for convenience…but what about marrying for money?

Eva Rutland continues her humorous look at reasons to say "I do!" in this delightful sequel to *Marriage Bait* and *The Wedding Trap*.

Books by Eva Rutland

HARLEQUIN ROMANCE®
2897—TO LOVE THEM ALL
2944—AT FIRST SIGHT
3064—NO ACCOUNTING FOR LOVE
3240—ALWAYS CHRISTMAS
3283—FOREIGN AFFAIR
3412—PRIVATE DANCER
3439—MARRIAGE BAIT
3490—THE WEDDING TRAP

The
Million-Dollar
Marriage
Eva Rutland

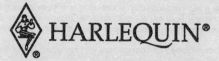

TORONTO • NEW YORK • LONDON
AMSTERDAM • PARIS • SYDNEY • HAMBURG
STOCKHOLM • ATHENS • TOKYO • MILAN • MADRID
PRAGUE • WARSAW • BUDAPEST • AUCKLAND

ISBN 0-373-03518-7

THE MILLION-DOLLAR MARRIAGE

First North American Publication 1998.

Copyright © 1998 by Eva Rutland.

Printed in U.S.A.

CHAPTER ONE

From her bedroom window, Melody Sands looked down at the man working in the rose bed. He moved with a quick energy that intrigued her. Clipping, digging, planting and transplanting like mad. As if he actually enjoyed it. In this weather! It was early March, but the winter winds were still going strong.

At least he's busy, she thought with a twinge of envy. Not rambling around in a big house that nobody lives in but Mrs. Cook, who, with a little outside help, keeps it in apple-pie order for Dad and me. In case either of us drop in, she thought, chuckling. She was only here now because she was bored with Dad's business ventures in Japan, bored with Adrian's relentless pursuit, and because there was no other place she particularly wanted to be. Nothing particular she wanted to do.

Oh, well...too rough for sailing, too windy for golf. Maybe something doing at the club.

She pulled on suede pants and a cashmere sweater, and went down to the kitchen.

"Hi, honey." Mrs. Cook, the cherubic house-keeper, looked up from the oversize thermos into which she was pouring hot coffee. "Ready for your coffee?"

Mel smiled as she nodded toward the thermos. "Not that much."

"Oh, I'm taking this to the man in the yard. I thought he could use a hot drink."

"New gardener?"

"No. Someone Pete hired to do whatever you do to roses this time of year. Pete's arthritis don't take to this weather. You want the usual juice and toast? I'll fix it as soon as I take this."

"I'll take it for you," Mel said, reaching for the thermos. She wanted to see that man close-up. "And don't bother about me. I'll get whatever I want. Okay if I borrow your jacket." Cook nodded, and she slipped on the well-worn oversize jacket, grabbed the thermos, and went out the back door.

He didn't see her approaching. He rested on his heels, intent upon what he was doing. She watched as he placed a rosebush in the ground, and with his bare hands arranged the soil around it, gently, with a kind of loving care.

"Hello," she said.

He looked up and she caught her breath. He was that handsome. Thick, unruly, very black hair, eyes almost as dark with thick, long lashes, features so perfect they might have been sculptured.

One quick graceful movement, and he was on his feet, dusting his hands on his jeans, laughing dark eyes looking down at her. "Hello. Something I can do for you?"

"No. Something for you," she said, still looking at him, holding on to the thermos with one hand while the other slapped at the hair whipping across her face. "Cook thought you might like a hot drink. It's so windy."

"Don't knock it. I like what it blew my way."

"Could be an ill wind," she quipped, trying to read the message in his eyes.

"Not when it blows in an angel," he said, as he caught a few flying strands of red hair, and inspected it. "Is this for real?"

"Take three guesses." She forced herself to break the spell and thrust the thermos at him. "Here," she said as she turned away.

"Hey, wait!" he called, almost dropping the thermos. "Don't blow away. Why don't you join me? You can have the cup. I'll drink out of the bottle."

She didn't want to leave. She turned back and accepted the hot drink he handed her. She sipped from the cup, feeling a little awkward.

He smiled at her. "I'm glad you stayed. Let's get acquainted. I'm Tony—"

"But I didn't come out here to get acquainted. Cook just asked me to..." She stopped. Cook hadn't asked her. She had volunteered. And now... The nerve of this guy!

"Tell Cook I'm mighty grateful, both for the coffee and the pretty angel who brought it."

"You're quite welcome, but I'm afraid you'll find I'm no angel."

His eyes brightened, his brows lifted. "You mean you've got a bit of devil in you? Interesting!"

This had gone far enough. She handed him the cup. "Thanks," she said, and turned away.

"Wait. I just want to get to know you. Anything wrong with that?"

"Yes. Not a mutual desire, since I've no wish to get to—"

"How would you know, if you never give me a chance? I'm not a bad guy."

"Look, I don't have time to dawdle here with you."

"Okay. I'm sorry. I didn't mean to hold you up. But, later... Couldn't we go somewhere? What time do you get off?"

"Off?" She was puzzled by the question.

"From that fancy joint." He gestured toward the house. "What time are you off work?"

Oh! He thinks I'm the maid. "I don't..." Whatever she intended to say was checked by his grin. An open, wholesome, boyish grin that lit up his whole face, and touched something deep inside her. Something that had lain dormant for a long time.

"I could pick you up. We could go for a burger or something, and...well, like I said, get acquainted.

How about it?''

She said nothing. Just kept watching him. Feeling a funny coming-alive feeling.

"Look, I'm an all-right guy. Really. Give me a chance.''

That crazy lopsided grin. Full lips curving around white, even... No. One tooth was crooked, lapping over another...

"Well, say something! Wouldn't you like to get to know me?''

"Not really," she lied. She liked that crooked tooth. He wasn't so darn perfect.

"Aw, come on. Why not?''

Why not? she echoed, wondering... Liking the laughter in his dark eyes.

"Look, it doesn't have to be a burger. You like pizza? Or there's this little Italian place down the valley. We could—''

"Six," she said.

"Huh?''

"Six o'clock. I'll be...ready then. Okay?''

"Okay!'' Jubilant, but wary, as if he couldn't believe his luck. "Shall I pick you up there?'' He nodded toward the back door.

"Sure.'' She turned to go. Couldn't stand there looking at him all day, could she!

"Okay! See you," he called after her. "Oh, and tell the cook thanks. I'll bring the thermos back before I leave.''

She rushed in, not daring to look back. What the hell had come over her? She didn't know this man from zilch. A gardener. Part-time gardener at that. Cheeky. And too good-looking. Probably had women falling all over him. For all she knew he could be some awful creep. He came on strong.

She laughed. Nothing creepy about that boyish grin, that open, honest... "Hey, give me a chance...I'm not a bad guy."

The crisp air must have whetted her appetite, for she shared an unusually hearty breakfast with Cook, absentmindedly responding to the housekeeper's cheerful chatter. Not once did she glance outside.

But his image stayed with her. The laughing, appraising dark eyes. That smile. The crooked tooth. His quick graceful movements.

When she was back in her room, she did look out. And was disappointed. He was gone.

Never mind. She would see him tonight, she thought, and was surprised by the jolt of anticipation.

Stupid. She didn't even know him. Had seen him for about...five minutes?

But the feeling of excited expectancy remained. She hadn't felt this way since... She swallowed, hating to admit it. Since Dirk...

She curled up on the window seat, and looked out into the yard again. It was raining now. A funny in-between-winter-and-spring rain. It had been winter when she met Dirk.

Dirk Johanson. Blond, blue-eyed Dirk Johanson, tall and...well, not movie-star handsome like... What was his name? Tom? No. Tony. But Dirk was striking, tall and muscular, so blond. He looked like a Viking or a Greek god, invulnerable against the high snow-covered cliffs. All the girls at the ski resort were wild about him. Me, too. And he chose me.

My head spun like crazy. I was all his. I would have gone to the end of the world with him...without one damn penny! I knew I would be safe in the loving and protective arms of this strong man. Hadn't I skied with him over Nevada's highest and most treacherous mountain slopes? A man who could conquer such mountains could...turn into a sneaking, conniving, self-serving, scurrying weasel when faced with the real world!

She didn't believe it. Even after he had deserted like the swine he was, she had waited. She had sat in that crummy motel room for three days...waiting. And, when her father came for her, she had vented her rage against him, not Dirk. How could Dad, who had never denied her anything, send Dirk away, threatening disinheritance if they carried out their plans to marry?

"He dumped you for a measly fifty thousand dollars," her father said. "He didn't care about you. It was your money."

She didn't believe him. It hurt too much. Even now.

She pressed her face against the window, and looked out. The fresh green leaves of early spring trembled and danced under the battering of the late winter wind and rain, but clung tenaciously to the tree boughs.

As she had clung to her faith in Dirk. She had slipped from the motel and evaded her father's detectives for three whole months. Even now she could smell the grease and cooking food in the Reno kitchens where she had washed dishes. Waitresses were too visible. She had called the Colorado ski resort and learned that Dirk had moved to a resort in Switzerland. Her letters to Switzerland were not answered, and she convinced herself that he never received them.

"Don't keep on being a fool!" Jake, her cousin, never bothered to cushion his words. Knowing her habits better than her father's detectives, he had traced her to that rooming house in Reno. "He got your letters, all right, just like he got that bundle from your dad! And he doesn't want you tailing him? Why do you think he hotfooted it to Switzerland?"

She stared at him, her mind fumbling for an excuse.

Jake bent toward her. "And why do you think he took that little hatcheck gal with him?"

"He didn't!"

"Oh, but he did."

She didn't want to believe that, either. But Jake had never lied to her. For that matter, neither had her father.

"Face it, Mel. Your dad did you a favor. You may as well swallow your stupid pride and come home."

She had gone home. How could she hold on to something that wasn't there!

"Forget him," Jake had said. And she vowed that she would.

But she had lost more than Dirk.

She had lost trust. The wonderful, exhilarating, fulfilling love found on the snow-covered slopes was a lie. Sold for fifty thousand dollars. Buried forever in the drab kitchens and cheap motel rooms in Reno.

Tony Costello slammed the door of his battered pickup truck, and ran up the steps of the modest bungalow on Lotus Street. The door was opened by Jerry, his seven-year-old nephew.

"Tony!" The little boy looked up in gleeful anticipation. "You come to help me with that model?"

"Not tonight. Got a date," Tony said, rumpling Jerry's hair as he followed him into a steamy, noisy kitchen.

"Hi, Tony. You're just in time. Sit over there by Patsy." His sister-in-law pointed with the spoon she was using to ladle out heavy servings of savory spaghetti. She was pretty, but heavy in the last stages of pregnancy, and her face and hair were wet with perspiration.

Tony bent over her bulging belly to kiss her cheek. "Thanks, Rosalie, but not tonight. I have a date, and I want to—"

"No!" his brother bellowed, almost choking on a mouthful of food.

"Aw, come on, Pedro!"

"Is it Joan?" Rosalie, who had filled her own plate, took her place at the table and smiled at Tony. "I like her. She's so—"

"Not Joan. Someone I just met. Well..." Almost met, he corrected to himself. He didn't even know her name. "Can't expect me to pick her up in my truck, can you?"

"Can if that's all you've got," Pedro said, moving just in time to prevent the kid in the high chair from dumping his dinner. "Watch it, buddy! It goes in your mouth, like this!"

"Aw, come on, Pedro," Tony said again, glancing at his watch. Almost five. And he still had to shower and shave. "Tell you what. I'll come over and break up the ground when you're ready to put in your vegetables." Pedro hated gardening more than he loved his '67 Mustang. That should do it.

Pedro was not about to give in easily. "If you'd get yourself a decent job, instead of monkeying around with flowers, you could buy your own ride. What kind of a living do you expect to make out of posies, for Pete's sake!"

"At least it's my own business. Which, I again remind you, has great potential. I'll be sitting back giving orders and collecting dividends, and you'll still be holding on to a jackhammer for fifteen bucks an hour."

"Twenty bucks. Which is why I've got a house and two cars, while you—"

"Did you bring me a present, Tony?" Patsy interrupted. She had heard this argument many times before.

"As a matter of fact, I did, honey." Tony tossed a bag of chocolates on the table. "Be sure to share it with your brothers."

"Not till after dinner," Rosalie said, confiscating the candy. "Who is this girl, Tony? Where did you meet her?"

"Around," was Tony's vague answer. "Come on, Pedro. I don't have time to argue. Where are the keys?"

Mel searched through her closet, trying to find something to wear. Armani suits and Calvin Klein dresses didn't exactly go with a burger stop or a pizza parlor. Maybe a simple wool dress. No. Pants, to climb into that beat-up truck he'd been driving. She pulled out a pair of brown wool pants and a matching sweater.

She had told Cook she did not want dinner, and had been glad to see her retire to her room before five. She wouldn't see her leave.

She was waiting in the kitchen when a vintage, shiny black Mustang motored down the drive. Not the truck she had expected.

It was him.

She slipped on her jacket and hurried out.

CHAPTER TWO

HE LOOKS different, too, she thought, as he got out
and came around to open the door for her. Rather
debonair, and more like a movie star than ever in
tan slacks and a cardigan sweater.

"Hello again," he said, his eyes lighting with
appreciation.

"Hello," was all the usually talkative Melody
could muster. Why, she wondered, did she feel so
giddy and light-headed?

"I thought we'd go to Beno's," he said as he
shifted gears and started down the driveway. "It's
not too far. Do you like Italian food?"

"Yes."

"Good." He smiled at her before turning into the
street. "Now that that's settled and we've howdied,
how about introducing ourselves? I'm Tony
Costello and you are...?"

"Melody Sands." Darn! Now he would know
who she was.

He didn't seem to make the connection. "Melody. Like a beautiful tune, huh?"

"A dumb name."

"Oh, I don't know. Melody," he mused. "I
kinda like it."

"I don't. I prefer just plain Mel."

"Okay. Mel. Have you always lived in Wilmington?"

"Mostly. At least, this is home."

"And I've never seen you before." He shook his head. "This must be my lucky day. How long have you been working for... Who lives there anyway?"

Was he putting her on? "Don't you know? You were working there."

"For Peter Dugan. He just asked me to do the rose beds at 18 Clayborn Drive."

"Oh." So he doesn't know who I am, she thought, pleased. She was...well, unencumbered. An ordinary girl on an ordinary date with an ordinary guy.

"I ought to pay him," he said.

"Who?"

"Pete."

"Why?"

He had pulled to a stop at a light, and turned to her. "I met you, didn't I?"

"Oh." She was mesmerized by the look in his dark eyes. Not laughing, but serious. As if seeing her as someone special.

"Guess I owe the cook, too. Best coffee I've ever tasted."

"Oh?"

"Maybe because you brought it. Do you know you have the brightest blue eyes and the most gor-

geous mop of red hair I've ever seen? Tell me, is
it for real?''

"You tell me," she said, at last finding her voice.
"Do you flirt so outrageously with all the women
you meet?''

"Only the pretty ones." There was that grin
again.

"And then?''

"Then what?" he asked, as he merged onto the
freeway.

"What do you do with the crowd? Do you select
the most beautiful one or do you take turns?''

"Ah, come on. I was kidding. I'm not some
fancy ladies' man. Really.''

He looked so embarrassed she couldn't help teasing him. "Then you'd better be careful, passing out
all that baloney. We poor females are vulnerable
creatures.''

"Bull. You're about as vulnerable as a stone
wall. And what I said wasn't baloney. You know
you're a number ten.''

She gave him a smug smile. "So I've been told.''

"I bet. Anyway, it was more than that…being
beautiful, I mean. You're…different." He gave her
a puzzled glance. "I don't understand it myself. I
don't usually go for this sort of thing.''

"What sort of thing?''

"This. A date. I don't have time. But this morning, when I saw you standing there…" He hesitated. "Well, it was like I didn't want to let you

get away. I wanted to know all about you. Who you are, what you do, what you like, what you don't like." Another quick glance. "So. What do you do all day up at that big house?"

"Oh, this and that," she said quickly, her throat suddenly dry. This was dangerous ground. "You promised I would get to know *you*. So tell me. What do you do besides fix rose beds for Pete?"

"Everything. Or maybe I should say anything…from weeding to landscaping."

"Oh?" She gave him a skeptical glance. Quite a gap between weeding and landscaping.

"Okay, here we are," he said, as he pulled into a crowded parking lot.

She looked at the unpretentious one-story building that didn't seem large enough to house all the occupants from the cars in the lot. It took him some time to find a parking slot. When at last he did, she reached for the door handle, but he was there before her.

"Hope we won't have to wait," he said as he opened the door and helped her out. Most polite man she had met in a long time. Even Adrian would have allowed her to hop out by herself. Maybe, she mused as he guided her toward the entrance, Adrian and his ilk were accustomed to a doorman helping her out when they drove up for valet parking.

Also, Adrian would have had a reservation, she thought when Tony apologized for the twenty-minute wait. "Hope you don't mind. I asked for a booth. So we can talk."

She didn't mind. In fact it was quite interesting, standing in the crowded entryway—it could hardly be called a lobby—watching people come and go. Like the fat man whom she thought was alone with his three noisy children until the harassed woman joined him, waving a doggie bag and exclaiming that Jimmie hadn't touched a thing on his plate, and she sure wasn't going to leave all that food. There was the overpainted woman holding on to a boy with bulging muscles who looked young enough to be her son. Was he her son? Hardly, not the way she was cuddling up to him. And the teenage girl with the ponytail who—

"Costello!" the man at the cash register shouted.

"Okay!" Tony said, taking her arm. "Wasn't too long, was it?"

Not long enough, she thought. She hadn't yet discovered who the teenager was with. She hoped she was with her parents. But as she followed Tony through crowded tables to a booth, she decided she was more interested in finding out about him.

"Are you a landscape artist?" she asked after the waitress had taken their order.

"Not bloody likely."

"But you said—"

"I lied."

"Shame on you," she said, laughing.

"To impress you."

"You wanted to impress me?"

"Sure. Why do you think I borrowed the car?"

"The Mustang? It's not yours?"

"Nope. Belongs to Pedro, my brother."

"Nice car. I enjoyed the ride. Thank him for me."

"Thank *me*. I'm doing the landscaping to pay for it."

"Oh. Then you really do landscaping?"

He grinned. "If turning up the soil for a vegetable garden qualifies."

"Oh, you!" The waitress brought their drinks, and Mel was silent for the moment, wondering why she wanted to know everything about this man. Obviously, he was a jack-of-all-trades, and she shouldn't embarrass him by pressing. She couldn't seem to help herself. "Will you stop trying to impress me and tell me what you really do?"

"Like I told you, everything. Okay, okay," he said, holding up a hand as if to ward off her scowl. "I'm in business for myself. And I only stretched the truth a bit. I've got two more years at the State in Landscape Architecture."

"Really? I am impressed."

"You needn't be. It's a long way off. Evening school only, because I have to keep working, and then I have to do an apprenticeship before I can get a license."

"But it sounds like a great career." She paused as the waitress set a plate piled with mounds of spaghetti before her. How was she to manage all that? she wondered, as she watched him expertly wind the spaghetti around his fork and begin to eat with relish. "I never can eat it like you're supposed to," she announced as she took her knife and cut small pieces, and sampled a forkful. "Delicious!"

"Yeah. Beno's special," he said.

"So, how did you happen to get into landscaping?" she asked.

"Grandma's rock garden."

"Come again?"

"Grandma wanted a rock garden and... Well, maybe it started before that. You see, I never wanted a nine-to-five job. At least not the kind my folks, Pop and both my brothers are into. Road construction. Guess I got a thing against concrete."

"Oh? That's a strange bias."

"Guess so, but there it is," he said. "Bugs me when good soil gets covered up. And we're getting closed in. Frank's got one of those new houses on Benton Circle. About an inch between him and his neighbors and not enough yard to spit in."

"Who's Frank?"

"That's my oldest brother."

"How many brothers do you have?"

"Just two."

"And a grandmother," she added to remind him. "Who wanted a rock garden."

"Yeah. My grandparents have this farm, a hundred and fifty acres, in Virginia, about an hour from here. Grandpa's not farming now. Bad case of arthritis. Anyway, there's not much profit since the big combines have taken over. He was about to sell it for a pile, but the developer ran into zoning problems, and backed down.'' Tony paused to take a swallow of beer. ''That was my lucky day.''

''Why so?''

''I talked Gramps into leasing to me.''

''But you said there was no profit—''

''In vegetables. Flowers are different.''

She put her fork down and stared at him. ''You're opening a florist shop?''

''Nope. A wholesale nursery. You see, I spent a lot of time on my grandparents' farm, and I just got into growing things. With all these acres of good rich soil—''

''Wait a minute. You said you're studying to be a landscape artist.''

''That came later with Grandma's rock garden.''

''I see. Meanwhile you're running a wholesale nursery.''

''Not yet. There's equipment to buy, greenhouses to build...things like that. Not to mention the plants themselves.''

''So you're actually planning two careers.''

''Not really. Don't you see how the two fit together?'' He began to talk of his plans with a boyish enthusiasm that intrigued her. The clatter of silver and the murmurs of other diners faded as she sat in the little booth and listened. Through his eyes she began to see hundreds of florists and supermarkets filled with lovely luscious and unusual plants from his nursery, landscapes green with the trees and shrubs that would break up the concrete surrounding houses, condominiums, even commercial buildings and shopping centers.

Melody Sands, bored up to the ying-yang with all the successful investments and mergers discussed by all the rich successful men she encountered, listened with deep interest and awe to the dreams of this young man who was starting on a shoestring. She liked being a Miss Nobody listening to an ordinary guy talk about... No. Nothing ordinary about this guy who was really a hunk, worked like a Trojan and dreamed big.

"I guess it will take some time," she said.

"And money," he said. "Why do you think I'm planting roses, cutting lawns, and having to borrow a car to impress the most fascinating woman I've ever met?"

"The *most* fascinating?" she teased.

"The most," he said with emphasis.

"Well, thanks for the flattery, but you didn't need a car to impress me. I could have ridden in the truck."

"You don't belong in a truck."

"How do you know where I belong?"

He didn't. And that's what bothered him. But he knew she didn't belong in a truck. From the moment he saw her, standing so erect, the wind whipping that mass of flaming red hair... He reached across the table to touch it. It felt like silk. "Is it for real?" he asked, just as he had the first time he saw it.

"Of course it's for real! Do you think I'd be fool enough to dye it this crazy color?"

"Not crazy. It's out of sight."

"Ha! If you knew how many times I've thought of dying it. A nice conservative brown or—"

"Don't you dare!" She jumped and even he was surprised at his vehemence. Why did he feel such possessiveness toward this woman he hardly knew?

Damn it, he didn't have time to possess any woman. Especially this one. Why did he sense she was out of his league? There was something about her. Something...well, classy. The way she carried herself with a certain confidence, maybe even arrogance. Even this morning, in that tattered jacket, her hair in disarray, she had looked...well, elegant. And so beautiful she took his breath away.

It's not the way she looks. It's the way she *is*. Warm, caring. Interested. He had sat all this evening spilling his guts. All his hopes and plans...things he had never even breathed to anyone else. And she had listened like they mattered to her.

This woman. This one woman. Why did he feel that he never wanted to lose her?

"Why are you looking at me like that?"

"Like what?"

"Like I might disappear or something?"

That was the way he was feeling. Scared. Like she might walk out of his life and he'd never see her again. This was crazy!

"Just thinking I'm pretty stupid," he said. "I want to know all about you, and I've spent all this time on me. Things I already know. So, tell me. How many brothers and sisters do you have, and where do you live, and when can I see you again?"

"Wait, you go too fast," she said, trying to get herself together. She didn't want to lie to this man. But she didn't want him to know who she was. She liked listening to him, almost as if she was sharing his dreams...like they were on the same level. Would he feel free to share if he knew? "I...I'm an only child," she said.

"I see. That explains that look."

"What look?"

"That I - can - have - anything - I - want - I'm - a - spoiled - brat look."

"Now, don't you start!" she said, feeling angry because she had always been accused of just that. "I'm not spoiled and I don't always get what I want." She hadn't gotten Dirk, had she? And never mind that he hadn't wanted her, just her money. She sat up, staring at Tony. He didn't know about the money. He liked *her*.

He was laughing. "Okay, don't bite my head off. I see you've got the temper that goes with that hair.

And I take it all back. You're not spoiled. You're working hard at...what do you do?''

"I...paperwork," she floundered. "For the man of the house." That was true. She often helped her father with his business.

"Oh, a secretary. I should have known." He reached for her hand with its perfectly polished nails. "Much too pretty and soft to do much scrubbing. And where do you live?''

"Where you saw me," she said, absorbed in the calloused thumb that was stroking the back of her hand, making her feel...like she hadn't felt for a long time.

"Oh, a live-in secretary?"

"Kinda."

"Don't know if I like that. You're much too pretty to be around some old fogy.''

"He's away. Away most of the time. He travels a lot.''

"Good. And your parents. Do they still live in Wilmington?''

"My mother's dead. And my father...well, we had a little disagreement." They had had a disagreement, hadn't they! "Anyway, he's away, working out of town.''

He could see that she was agitated by his probing, so he let up. There would be time. "Better take you home, much as I hate to," he said. "I've got to start early in the morning.''

CHAPTER THREE

SHE couldn't sleep. She was too keyed up. Still glowing from the most exciting evening she had spent in years.

She laughed at herself. What, for Pete's sake, was so exciting about sitting in a crowded little restaurant, struggling with a plateful of slippery spaghetti?

Just talking. They had talked all the way back to the house, where he got out of the car and stayed with her until she let herself in. Protective, courteous. Too courteous. He hadn't kissed her.

Because of the outside lights? Because he didn't want to?

She felt like she had been kissed. So alive, tingling as in after a night of passionate lovemaking.

Was it because he had asked when he could see her again? Hell, every man she ever dated asked that. Why was Tony Costello different? Why had she wanted to shout... "Tomorrow, the next day, and the next. Anytime! Anywhere!" She wanted to pin down a time. She had told him not to call the house because she wasn't sure what kind of signal Mrs. Cook would give off. She had thought of confiding in her. The housekeeper went a long way back and had always been warm and friendly toward her, but she was also loyal to Dad. During the Dirk episode, Mel had never known which side she was on. Best not to confide.

Confide? Good Lord, this wasn't a conspiracy or anything like that! She was going to tell Tony all about herself, wasn't she?

When?

Soon.

How soon?

When we get to know each other…well, better. When it won't matter.

It matters now?

To me, it does. Because Tony likes me. *Me.* Not who I am. At least he doesn't know who I am, and I think he likes me.

Anyway, I like him. So much that I can't stand to see him leave without knowing when I'll see him again.

So it was she who had said, "What are you doing tomorrow evening?" Then wanted to bite her tongue because he looked so surprised. She was surprised herself. Usually it was her escort, not she, who was eager.

"I have school," he said. "I missed tonight. Can't afford to miss too much. What about Sunday?"

"Good," she said, disappointed. Four days away. "We can go on a picnic. I'll fix us a lunch."

He looked embarrassed. "I meant Sunday night.

You see, Sunday is my only day off and the only time I get to work at the farm.''

''You weren't kidding, were you?''

''Huh?''

''You really don't have time to date.''

''Not until you,'' he said with such emphasis that her breath caught. He did like her! ''Sunday night? We could take in a movie or go dancing. Whatever you like.''

''You said you work at the farm,'' she said, absorbed in his eyes. They seemed to promise…something. ''Why…I mean, what do you do out there all day?''

''Lots of things. And…well, right now I've got a few lilies ready for the Easter market. Got to fix them for delivery on Monday.''

''Need some help?''

''Now you're kidding.''

''No, I'm not. I could help you plant or hand you things…whatever.'' Anything. Just so she could be with him. ''Anyway, I want to see your grandma's rock garden.''

He was silent for a moment and she couldn't tell what he was thinking. She breathed a sigh of relief when he finally said, ''You don't know what you're in for. But…okay, it's a deal!''

And now she was so excited she couldn't sleep. She got out of bed, walked to the window and looked out at the night. How could she wait till Sunday?

And she'd have to confide in Cook. No way could she explain being picked up in a truck early Sunday morning.

"Damn it! You got the car, didn't you! You said you'd turn the soil and..."

Tony held the phone away from his ear, but Pedro's tirade came through loud and clear. "I didn't say this weekend."

"You said when I was ready. I'm ready."

"Ah, come on, Pedro. I got a date...sorta."

"What do you mean...sorta?"

"Another date, Tony?" Rosalie broke in.

"Oh, hi, Rosie. Didn't know you were on the line."

"Hi. Just picked up to call Mom and heard you and Pedro squabbling. Gee, Tony, you had a date the other night. Again today? That's good. You haven't had a date in months. Same girl or—"

"Will you get off the phone, Rosie! This jerk's trying to wiggle out. You heard him! He said—"

"Okay, okay! Tomorrow. Early." Tony slammed down the phone. Wouldn't take more than half an hour to do Pedro's little plot, but he was already going to lose three hours at the farm. Couldn't expect Mel to get up at the crack of dawn, could he? Mel...beside him all day. Hell and damnation, he'd lose more than three hours. He grimaced, but could not shake thrill of anticipation. Neither could he shake the feeling that she didn't belong in a truck.

She was dressed for it when he stopped for her the next morning. Even if those jeans did look as if she had been poured into them. Her loafers were scuffed, the yellow pullover faded, and that gorgeous hair was tied back with a yellow scarf. Suddenly the sun was brighter, the air more refreshing, the day crisp and rich with promise.

He laughed as he lifted her into the truck. "You're worth three hours," he said. Just the sight of her was worth a whole darn day.

"What are you talking about? I'm ready, at eight, just like you said, aren't I?"

"Right. Don't mind me. I'm mad because Pedro's cutting into my prime time, and I'm taking it out on you."

"Pedro? The owner of the Mustang?"

"Who's demanding payment pronto!"

"Oh, yes. The...er...landscaping. I take it his yard is bigger than your other brother's. What's his name?"

"Frank. Yeah, Pedro bought one of those old houses in Richmond. East End."

An alarm bell sounded. Mel gasped. Wasn't that the section where Jake's wife's company was doing a lot of business? If she ran into Judy...

Oh, for goodness' sake, Judy might be a dedicated architect/contractor, but was surely at home now, very much occupied with their two-week-old son. Oh, hell, Judy wouldn't be hobnobbing with the residents, would she? Not even anywhere in the area on a Sunday, and...

And I'm getting paranoid. This is ridiculous. I should just tell Tony who I am.

"Used to be a pretty bad section." Tony, who seemed not to notice her reaction, was still talking. "They're upgrading it now, and Pedro got a real bargain. Not bad. Big yard, trees."

"That's good."

"Yeah. More breathing space than the new ones like Frank's."

"Space enough for vegetable gardens than need tilling, huh?" Why not tell him? What difference would it make?

"Right. But it won't take long. And it's on the way to the farm."

"Does Pedro have children?" That's when she'd tell him. On the drive to the farm. It would be awkward, but... Oh, well, just a misunderstanding. Not worth mentioning. Didn't seem important, forgot.

"He has three, and one on the way. You'll meet them."

She did meet them. All at once. They converged upon the truck as soon as it rolled around the house into the backyard. A boy and girl who jumped from a tree and came running. A dark-haired pregnant woman with a toddler squirming in her arms.

Tony jumped down and took the boy from her. "You shouldn't be lifting him, Rosie."

"I didn't want him to run under your truck. He

heard you turn into the drive and was off!'' The woman spoke to Tony, but her wide speculative eyes were on Mel.

Uncomfortable under the inspection, she smiled. "I'm Mel," she said, glancing at Tony. He was involved with the children who were climbing all over him. "I hope you don't mind my tagging along."

"I'm Rosalie, and I don't mind at all. I'm delighted. You can keep me company while they work."

The screen door slammed, and a man came out. Pedro, of course. A slightly heavier version of Tony, almost as good-looking. "Get off Tony," he shouted. "He's here to work, not to play with you."

Tony, relieved of the children, made the introductions, including the kids. "Patsy, Jerry and Mike, better known as Buddy."

As they were exchanging greetings, another man came across the lawn. A tall lean man.

"Charlie Hill, my neighbor," Pedro said. "This is Melody Sands, Charlie, a friend of Tony's."

Mel's heart jumped into her throat. She knew this man. She had met him at Jake's just last week, when he and his wife came to bring a present for the new baby. Did he recognize her?

His look said he did. But evidently he had also caught the slight shake of her head, for he simply acknowledged the introduction as if he had never seen her before. She thanked him with her eyes, wanting to explain that it would be all right as soon as she told Tony who she was.

Tony was taking down a machine, and talking to Charlie about some plants he wanted. Mel, still a little shaken, found she was being addressed by the little girl.

"Tony's got to work," Patsy explained. "You want to play with us?"

Mel looked down, delighted by the wide, friendly, one-tooth-missing smile. "What are you playing?"

"We're pirates. That's our ship." The boy pointed to a wooden platform that had been constructed along two limbs of the wide-spreading cedar tree.

"Can you climb a tree?" Patsy asked.

"Sure," Mel answered. She had ridden horses, sailed boats, skied steep mountain slopes. But…she had never climbed a tree in her life. It seemed a good idea. "I'd enjoy it," she assured the apprehensive Rosalie.

"Well, only for a few minutes. Then it's my turn. Women talk," Rosalie added, and winked at Mel before going into the house.

Mel was glad she had opted for the tree. She wasn't ready for Rosalie's "women talk." Not until the coming talk with Tony.

Following Jerry's instructions, she mounted the two-stair step boards that had been driven into the trunk of the tree and swung easily onto the first big limb. The platform was sturdy with ample space for the three of them, and, with a bit of pretend, was a ship tossing upon an ocean far below.

"I'm the captain, and Patsy's first mate," Jerry announced. "You can be the second mate," he generously conceded.

"Aye, aye, sir." Mel saluted, and following orders, climbed to the "masthead" to sight vessels within capturing distance. The weather had turned warm, but there was a gentle breeze stirring. The top of the tree swayed in the breeze, and Mel held on, viewing the vast ocean of fenceless backyards that stretched below her. There was Tony expertly handling the noisy rototiller that was uprooting the garden soil several yards from the house. There was Pedro directing Tony and making sure a scampering Buddy was kept safely away from the machine. There was a blue fenced-in unoccupied swimming pool in the yard next door. "Belongs to the Hills," Jerry had said, "but we can swim in it anytime...that is, when Charlie's there to watch us."

Charlie, who knew who she was. For goodness' sake, she was acting like being rich was a crime! And it wasn't like she was trying to deceive Tony. She planned to tell him this afternoon, as soon as she got the chance!

She took a deep breath and continued to survey the neighborhood. Two houses away, three teenage boys tossed a basketball at a hoop mounted on the back of the garage. There was the sweet smell of cedar mingling with the fresh aroma of newly over-turned earth.

There was a vague sad sense of something she had missed. A yard that blended into other people's yards where other children played and shared swimming pools and basketball hoops. Hers had been a big yard that stretched for acres, and contained no child but herself. Plenty of trees, but not one to climb. Or was it she had not thought of climbing? Would it have been permitted? Visions of her childhood flashed before her. Coloring books, games, or puzzles with whichever nanny. Contact with other children was restricted to birthday parties or visits to the club under the careful supervision of several nannies. Less supervision when she graduated to horses and boats, of course.

But she envied these children who, even in their early years, had the freedom to imagine and pursue their own games. She enjoyed every precious minute with them. She was sorry when Rosalie called that breakfast was almost ready. Jerry was to tell the men and Patsy should come to set the table.

"We'll do this another time," she told the children. She would take them sailing on a real boat…Jake's. They would like that.

After the ritual of hand-washing, Mel followed Patsy into a big kitchen which smelled delicious. "Can I help?" she asked.

"No, indeed. Everything's about ready," Rosalie

declared. "You just sit over here and talk to me while Patsy sets the table."

When I was Patsy's age, Mel thought, I wasn't even allowed in the kitchen, where a Swedish cook, at one time a French chef, presided. She watched in amazement as the little girl set out the plates, silver, coffee mugs, glasses, and paper napkins as efficiently as her mother turned over the hash browns.

"Is Wilmington your home?" Rosalie asked as she added slices of red onions to the potatoes.

"Yes."

"Lived here all your life?"

"Mostly." She was right. Rosalie was curious.

"Me, too. Lacey Elementary and Milton High. Did you go to Milton?"

Mel shook her head, visions of her Swiss finishing school dancing through it.

Rosalie laughed as she stirred the onion rings in with the potatoes. "Don't know why I keep thinking I should have seen you somewhere. If you had gone to Milton, it would have been long after me. Good gracious, seems a hundred years since my high school days. Patsy, strap Buddy in his chair, and see if the men are getting washed up. Oh, here they are."

Just in time, Mel thought, with a sigh of relief. She was glad Rosalie's turn with her had been brief. Answering the inquisition would have been awkward. After she told Tony...

After a brief but solemn blessing by Pedro, the usual Sunday ritual began...a short Bible verse from each person at the table. Mel panicked. Her church excursions were skimpy. Her mind frantically searched. Please, she prayed as, beside her, Patsy's child voice confidently crooned, "Honor thy father and thy mother..."

Her prayer was answered. Her mother's funeral. She repeated the pastor's words. "In my Father's house are many mansions..." Thank you, she silently whispered to a God she hardly knew.

It was a good thing that everybody in this family was very active. Otherwise they would all be fat, Mel thought as the full platters were passed around. Potatoes browned to perfection and well seasoned by the crispy onions. Thick, juicy slices of ham. Hot biscuits with jam or honey, eggs to order, and strong, hot coffee. Rosalie was obviously in the last stages of pregnancy, but even she could not be called fat. Probably never would be, Mel thought, the way she kept jumping up and down to serve everyone. Every now and then Patsy was called upon for hot biscuits or to get more butter. But no man, not even little Jerry, budged. Meals were definitely women's work.

It was a hilarious gathering, with everyone, even the children, talking at once. About everything, from the vegetables Pedro was going to plant to the "owie" on little Buddy's skinned knee. Mel said nothing, but felt warm and happy, a part of the camaraderie. Happy listening to down-to-earth talk that had nothing to do with stock options or how the market was going. Happy just looking at Tony.

He was beautiful. Now that was stupid. Calling a man *beautiful*, especially one as masculine as Tony. Tall, and yes, almost too slender, but with strong rippling muscles that made him seem as sturdy as a tree trunk. She loved the way he used those muscles with graceful dispatch. Planting roses, or lifting her into his truck as if she was as light as a feather. She loved the tender caring way he had taken Buddy from Rosalie, the easy strength with which he had held the rototiller steady. How he was laughing at something Pedro had said, and that crooked tooth was showing. She loved that crooked tooth, loved the way he ate. With his fork in his left hand! Why? He wasn't European. Funny, she had not noticed at the spaghetti house. Just that he had wound the spaghetti around his fork with the same ease and dispatch as he did everything else. She loved the way he moved.

She loved him.

This was ridiculous. She didn't really know him. Hadn't known he existed five days ago.

He had never even kissed her. None of those passionate, all-consuming, erotic sensations that had once rippled through her body on a Nevada mountaintop. A love she had lost and never hoped to find again.

This couldn't be it, could it? Couldn't love a man

just because he held his fork in his left hand and handled a rototiller with ease, could she?

But there it was. A warm, sure knowing. A feeling that she had found someone wonderful, someone warm, caring and dependable. A feeling that she had come home to a man she would love forever.

Come home to...? Good heavens! What made her think he would have these same crazy mixed-up impossible sensations!

She tried to get back on track, and focused on the conversation at the table.

Pedro's deep laugh bellowed out. "Married into money, did he?"

"Guess so. More'n he'd ever had, anyway," Tony said. "She's got some kind of catering business that's beginning to pay off."

"So you lost the only employee in your little posy business."

Mel didn't like the way Pedro said that. Like he was putting Tony's business down.

Tony didn't seem to mind. He answered readily enough. "Wasn't much help anyway, the lazy slob."

"What's his wife like, Tony?" Rosalie wanted to know.

"Busty blonde. Kinda good-looking, but a bit bossy for my taste. Joe'll be dancing to her tune the rest of his life."

"But he's pretty well set, ain't he?" Pedro's

laugh rang out again. "Maybe you should follow Joe's example, Tony. If you're gonna stick with posies, you could use some support."

"No thank you. I prefer to dance to my own tune."

"Atta boy!" Pedro slapped his brother on the back. "You might be a posy peddler, but you're a Costello all the way, right?"

"Right," Tony agreed.

"Yep, we Costello men support our women. They don't support us." Pedro now addressed his remarks to Mel. "My little Rosalie hasn't worked a day since she married me."

Mel smiled and nodded an approval which she didn't exactly feel. It looked as if Rosalie was working her head off right now.

But she had just learned something important. About somebody named Joe, and about Costello men.

Maybe she shouldn't tell Tony she was rich. Not yet.

CHAPTER FOUR

"You love the farm, don't you?" Mel asked as Tony merged the truck onto the freeway.

"Yeah. It's...well, kinda home base for all I plan to do." His face brightened as he began to talk of his plans, how he would divide each plot, where he would set out the trees, which would be reserved for the greenhouses. "All that rich soil. It's a perfect place for a nursery, and I'm itchy to get started. But I have to go slow. It'll take quite a bit of capital to set it up right."

"You could borrow." Every venture her father went into was on somebody else's money, not his.

"Can't borrow without security."

"The land..."

"Belongs to my grandparents, the only security they have. Grandpa was running into debts the last few years, but he never borrowed. I think they were sorry when the sale didn't go through, but with the present zoning laws, they wouldn't get enough to sustain them. They're leasing it to me for peanuts, but I plan to make it up to them when I get going." His voice rang with confidence and determination. She felt in her heart that it wouldn't be long before he "got going."

44

"Do you spend much time out there?" she asked.

"Not as much as I'd like to. Got a room in town near the school and more convenient for the jobs I pick up."

"But you'd rather be at the farm?"

"Oh, sure. And I stay there as much as I can. Still have my old room."

"Your old room? You spent a lot of time there as a kid?"

"Every summer."

"Your brothers, too?"

"Only me. Frank and Pedro were into baseball and wouldn't leave the city, and Marie was too little."

"Marie?" This was the first she had heard of a sister.

"Baby of the family, and the only girl. She's at City College now. Really into drama, which bugs the hell out of Pop."

"Why? If she enjoys it..."

"Wrong crowd for his little girl." Tony grinned. "Guess Pop must have read one or two of those wild stories about actresses in *People* magazine."

"Oh." Mel wondered if Tony's family really lived in the twentieth century. His grandparents must be out of this world. And she was about to meet them. No wonder she had the jitters.

But the jitters began to dissipate as they left the city noise and traffic for the comparatively uncrowded countryside. There was something magically calming about the quiet, the smell of country air, the sight of rolling green pastures and acres of freshly tilled earth.

"Here we are," Tony said as he turned the truck into a tree-shaded lane. The lane led to a two-story clapboard house that seemed small under three towering oaks. There was a banistered porch that wrapped around the house. There was a frisky dog that ran across the lawn to meet them.

There was the feeling that she had come home to something warm, solid and enduring. Strange. She tried to understand it as she jumped down to pet the dog that greeted them with excited barks.

Suddenly the peace was broken by a woman's voice, frantic, cutting through the yelps of the dog. "Tony! Thank God. Come quick!"

Tony sprinted into the house, Mel following, somewhat impeded by the dog. By the time she entered the wide living room, Tony was kneeling beside a large man who was sprawled across the four steps of a landing which led to a steep stairway. A small woman also knelt beside him, and the dog was licking his face.

The man was cursing. "Damn it! I'm all right I tell you. Down, Cocoa down! Damn it, Tony, get this fool mongrel the hell off me!"

"Just keep still, Al. Is he hurt?" The woman anxiously questioned Tony who seemed to be checking for broken bones.

"Hell! I keep telling you I'm not. If somebody would take this damn fool dog and give me a hand..."

Mel scooped up the damn fool dog who struggled in her arms trying to get to his master.

"Okay, Gramps, take it easy. Hold on to me." As the woman stood back, Tony, relieved of the encumbrances, managed to lift his grandfather to his feet. Mel marveled at the ease with which he held the much larger man, the gentleness with which he settled him on the sofa. "Are you okay, Grandpa?" he asked. "Can I get you something?"

"Get some sense in his head." Mrs. Costello's voice was sharp with anger, but she dabbed at tears with an unsteady hand. "He's stubborn as a mule. He knows he needs help on those stairs."

Mel, seeing she was near the breaking point, moved toward her. "Why don't you sit down? And maybe...Tony, is there some brandy?"

"Oh, honey, I don't need a thing." For the first time she noticed Mel. "For goodness' sake, put Cocoa outside."

Mel looked down at the silky milk-chocolate coat of the spaniel in her arms. Cocoa, of course. She rushed to the screen door, and shut the dog out. When she returned, Tony was holding a glass of water to the older man's lips.

Mr. Costello took a sip, then brushed it away. "Stop fussing over me, boy! Like I'm some feeble lamebrain slob."

"That's exactly what you are. I've been telling you and telling you not to try to come downstairs without—"

"Damn it! I wasn't coming down. I was going up…to get my other glasses. And what's all the fuss about? Any damn fool can slip."

Mrs. Costello was about to continue with her remonstrances, but Tony broke in. "Don't worry, Grandma. He's okay. Look, this is Melody Sands. She came out here especially to see your rock garden. Why don't you go out and show it to her? I'll get Grandpa's other glasses and I'll take these in to be fixed tomorrow," he added as he picked up the glasses and began to clear up the bits of the broken lens.

It took some persuasion, but finally Mrs. Costello led Mel through the hall and out to view the backyard. "Nothing here but Bermuda grass and that old apple tree before Tony took over," she explained. "It's early, but some of the flowers are in bloom. In midsummer, it's spectacular."

"It's spectacular now," Mel said. A long stretch of lush green grass was bordered by boxed shrubs and flower beds. At the very end of the yard, a slope led up to a lattice-covered gazebo. The rock garden was embedded in this slope, which was even now ablaze with color. Red, yellow, purple, pale pink and lavender buds peeked through ferns and rocks of various dimensions. A circular stone staircase led to the gazebo. They climbed them and sat in wrought-iron chairs to look down at the garden.

"It's so natural," Mel said. "Like the plants are growing wild around those rocks."

"They are wildflowers for the most part," Mrs. Costello said, "but each plant was carefully placed by Tony. Every stone and every drainage pipe. He said if he didn't get the drainage right, the yard would always be flooded. So he dug into those books." She shook her head. "He got more out of the rock garden than I did, with all that studying and planning. That's what gave him the landscaping bug."

"So he told me," Mel said. They sat for a long time, enjoying the beauty and talking about Tony. Tony, who had read, planned, carefully placed every stone and flower to create that beauty.

Later, when Mrs. Costello went in to "see after my husband," Mel went in search of Tony.

"You'll find him in the barn," Mrs. Costello told her, and Mel walked toward that tall wooden unimposing structure.

At the entrance of the cool, dim interior, she halted, catching her breath, struck by what she saw. Blooming plants...as far as the eye could see. Row upon row of potted plants stretched on long tables covering almost every inch of the barn's first floor.

She blinked. Closed her eyes. Opened them. Focused on a sea of white and pink. Lilies in pots of various sizes.

"Oh, Tony, they're lovely," she breathed. "And, golly...so many! There must be thousands."

"Not quite. Maybe about three hundred. And I think I've got enough orders for the whole lot." He explained that a smart wholesaler should always be prepared for the season. "Poinsettias for Christmas, lilies for Easter, and long-stem roses forever," he said, grinning. "I've been nursing these lilies since last fall. I'm starting delivery tomorrow, and this," he said, tapping the can, "will keep them fresh and alive for the whole season." He did not look up from his task. Patiently and rapidly he moved from plant to plant with his huge watering can.

"This will take you all afternoon," she said. "Don't you have another can?"

"So you really are going to help! Okay!" He hastily filled another can, carefully measuring water and the feeding substance, but looked dubious as he handed the huge can to her. "Can you lift it?"

"I'm stronger than you think," Mel answered, lifting the can. A cinch for a woman who had hoisted many a sail for Jake's Nantucket races.

They were both busy at work when Mrs. Costello slipped into the barn. "Tony, I have to talk to you."

Mel put down her watering can. "I'll just step outside."

"Oh, honey, keep on with your work. I know Tony wants to get these to market and I'm glad you're helping. Since Joe deserted, he's all by himself. Anyway, this may be family business, but it's surely not private. We're all holding our breath over this zoning, some wanting it to go one way and some the other. But…'' She sighed and turned to Tony. ''I'm sorry, Tony. I wanted to hold on for you, but it looks like I can't wait. We need to sell as quickly as we can. This man from Ray Realtors called last week. He's not offering what we want, but maybe we should take him up on it.''

Mel picked up her watering can and turned away. She didn't want to see Tony's face. But she heard every word of the conversation that followed.

''You saw your grandpa today. He can't take those stairs.'' The stairs were crucial, as the only full bath was upstairs. It would cost a small mint to install a tub or even a shower in the powder room downstairs. Anyway, at this point they both needed the partial care available at the nearby senior citizens facility.

''I've been looking into it,'' she said. ''And the truth is we can't afford it, unless we sell. I haven't said a word to Al. It's going to be hard to get him to leave this place.'' Her voice broke. ''Hard on me, too, Tony. We both love it here, and we wanted to keep it for you.''

Tony put his arms around her. ''Don't worry about me. All your life you have given to me. Now it's time we looked after you. Of course you should sell, and maybe you can get a better deal…just on the potential. The zoning change is almost inevitable. I'll check with some other Realtors tomorrow.

And, buck up," he said, kissing her cheek. "We knew you'd eventually have to sell, and I'm worried about Grandpa, too." He kept reassuring her that things would work out for all of them. In the meantime, he'd give up his place in town and stay here to help out with his grandfather. "I'll be here as much as I can, and always overnight until we work things out."

Mel kept working, but it took all the willpower she could muster to keep her mouth shut. She wanted to swing around and tell them she could fix everything. She could have a master bedroom and two full baths installed downstairs, and she could hire as much help as they needed. Or she could buy the farm outright for money enough for the older couple to live wherever they wanted, as long as they wanted. And Tony could have this beautiful peaceful place to do with it what he willed.

None of it would make a dent, not even in the interest from the trust fund received from her grandmother when she was twenty-one. Not to mention the hefty allowance from her father.

But... "We Costello men support our women. They don't support us."

A hot flush burned her cheeks. *Our women?*

Good Lord! Was she thinking of herself as Tony's woman? Tony, whom she'd known not quite a week! Tony, who had not given one sign...who had never even kissed her!

No, she wasn't his woman so she needn't worry

about that. But, otherwise they would consider it charity, and she knew they wouldn't accept that, either.

Still, there must be something she could do. She'd talk to Jake.

"Finished with all but this row? Good girl! You've sure been a help. Here, let me finish."

Mel became aware that Mrs. Costello had gone, and Tony, having finished his, was taking over her job. He didn't look nearly as upset as she had expected him to be. "Tony, I heard what your grandmother said. I'm sorry."

He shrugged. "Inevitable. And probably better now than later. Particularly after I will have set out trees and erected greenhouses."

She stared at him. "I see what you mean."

"Yeah. Stupid to put so much into something that could be sold out from under me at any time."

"I see what you mean," she said again. But plans were skidding through her mind. She would talk to Jake.

"It's my grandparents I'm really worried about. They need help. They could move in with Mom and Pop, but they've got too much pride for that. Anyway, the way Grandma talked they might be pretty happy at the senior citizens place. More activity than they have here by themselves, and it seems some of their friends have already moved there. I'll get in touch with a Realtor tomorrow."

And she would get in touch with Jake.

"I'll start loading up later," Tony said. "I'd better see to my roses now. Why don't you go in with Grandma?"

"No, I'll help you," she said, chuckling as she remembered Cook's words, "Doing whatever you do to roses this time of year."

She was surprised at the extent of his rose bed.

"My long-stem prizes," he said. "Several varieties. Don't have the greenhouse yet for all-year-round, but these constitute my main income during the summer months."

She noticed a small bed which was some distance from the others, and was enclosed with wire fencing. "Why are these separate?"

"I'm doing some experimenting," he said. Then he frowned, and for a moment did look a little upset. "Hope I can finish it before they sell."

"What can I do?" she asked.

He put down his tools and took both her hands in his. "Beautiful," he said, gazing a long time at her soft, slender fingers, the perfectly manicured nails. "And I want them to stay that way." He lifted each hand to his lips, kissed each in a courtly manner. "So why don't you just stick around and keep me company while I work."

She wanted to be good company, and pulled out every anecdote she could think of to keep him laughing while he transplanted, pruned and whatever. She watched him, delighted by his laughter, fascinated by the graceful precise way he worked, loving the sweet, warm tingling sensation that still radiated through her from the hands he had kissed.

He did let her hold the hose to water the beds he had fed. By that time, Mrs. Costello called them in to dinner. A simple but delicious dinner...roast lamb, parsleyed potatoes and tiny green peas. A cheerful dinner, with no talk about a farm to be sold or crippling arthritis.

After dinner, when Tony went out to load the truck, Mel followed.

"You'd better let me do this," he said. "Some of these pots are heavy."

"Nonsense," said the girl who had hoisted sails, saddled horses, and skied steep mountain slopes. She worked right with him.

"I've got to wrap some of these," Tony said when they had half the truck loaded. "The florist shops like to do their own, but the grocery stores I've contacted like them to come already dolled up."

"You don't seem to be very good at dolling up," she said when she saw him fumble with the colorful tinfoil and ribbons he had purchased. "I'm taking this over." She took the scissors from him and thoroughly enjoyed making her artistic wrappings. They made a good team, she wrapping and he loading.

"I haven't known you very long, Tony Costello," she said when they had finished. "But on this one Sunday, I've learned at least one thing about you."

"What's that?"

"You never stop working."

She watched his eyes fill with laughter. "I see," he said. "And I've learned something about you."

"And that is?" she asked, holding her breath. What did he really think about her?

"That you are the most industrious, most delightful, most exhilarating companion one could have."

"Why, thank you, sir," she said, breathing easier.

"And I'd like you to know more about me," he said.

"Oh? Like what?" she asked.

"Like this." It was then he kissed her. And there, in the cool, dim barn, a raging fire burst within her. A passionate, hungry, yearning fire that was never to be quenched. A titillating, exhilarating flame of desire. But there was more than passion in the strong gentle arms that enfolded her, more than desire in the taut muscled body that pressed close, the lips that teased and caressed. There was a message, a warm sure knowing. She had come home...to something wonderful.

CHAPTER FIVE

MEL was at Jake's house before breakfast the following morning. She found him in the nursery with his wife and baby. Judy, his wife, held the baby over her shoulder and was gently rubbing his back. She had the harried appearance of a new mother whose whole attention is focused on her child. The crisply ruffled negligee that matched her green eyes was rumpled and spotted from the baby's nursing, her lovely mass of golden hair was disheveled and carelessly tied back, and her face was devoid of makeup. She looked beautiful, flushed pink and positively glowing with happiness. Her husband could hardly take his eyes from her.

"Proud of yourselves, aren't you? Produced the great son and heir, huh?" Mel teased. "Well, let me get a look at him for goodness' sake. Let me hold him."

"Wait till he burps," Judy said. When she was rewarded by a belch from the child, she smiled in relief and handed him over.

"You're too beautiful to be a boy," Mel said, hugging him to her. "And your name is too big for you, Jacob Wellington Mason, the Fourth."

"Jake said the first one is always named Jacob,"

Judy said, as she removed a teddy bear and smoothed the sheet on the crib.

"The first?" Mel glanced at her cousin. "How many do you plan to have?"

Jake winked. "About a dozen. Nine at least. Enough for a baseball team."

His wife threw the teddy bear at him. He caught it, laughing. "Okay, a basketball team. That's only five."

"Pretty hard on a working wife, isn't it?" Mel asked.

"Part-time worker," Jake said. "You should take a look at her new office, right across from the den downstairs."

"Where you can keep an eye on her, huh?"

"And where she can keep an eye on my boy. Give him to me. That's not the way to hold him."

Mel watched him pace the floor, crooning softly to the baby on his shoulder. She was touched. Jake had always been a bit of a playboy, never the domestic type. But he sure was domestic now. And likely to stay that way, she thought, watching Judy's fond gaze on her husband. She'd probably have the dozen kids if he wanted them.

When the baby fell asleep and was safely tucked in his crib, Mel turned a serious face to Jake. "I need to talk to you."

"Thought so," he said. "Any time you show up before breakfast... Let's eat while we talk. I'm starving."

"Am I invited?" Judy asked.

"Oh, sure." Mel put an arm around her. "I need your input, too."

"Well, I'm glad about that," Judy said, with a teasing smile. "I'm still jealous of you. You're pretty darn close, for just a plain old cousin."

Mel thought about that as they trooped downstairs. Judy was right. Jake had always been closer to her than anyone else, even her parents who had been totally involved with each other. When her mother died, her dad had turned to business. No siblings, no cousins on her father's side, and only Jake on her mother's. He was six years older than she, but had never seemed to mind when she tagged along, whether he was sailing, swimming, or on horseback. In every crisis of her life, he had always been there.

"What's up now?" he asked, when they were all seated at breakfast.

She told him about "an elderly couple who owned a farm that they didn't want to sell, only they needed the money."

"It doesn't seem right," she said. "When a person has worked hard all his life, he ought to have enough to live comfortably when he gets so he can work no longer."

"Feeling guilty?" Jake asked.

"Huh?"

"About people who never work, but have the money to do whatever they want all their lives?"

"Well...since you put it that way..." She looked at Jake who had more millions than anyone in the family. For the first time, she thought she understood his tendency for indiscriminate giving. To tell the truth, she had never thought much about money, one way or the other. Until now.

"So what do you want to do?" Jake asked. "Buy the farm?"

"No! I can't. That is, I don't want him to know I have anything to do with it."

"Oh. You want me to buy it?"

"No. I don't want anyone to buy it. He needs it."

"He?"

"A...friend. A relative of the couple."

"Okay, Mel. Stop beating around the bush and tell me what's up."

So she told them. Everything. "And he really is just a friend. He doesn't even know who I am, and I don't want him to know. Not yet."

Judy looked at her husband. She said this Tony Costello sounded like a very industrious young man. She said she knew how it was to start out on a shoestring, and she came up with the solution. Her company could take an option on the place. Mel could give the money to Jim, Judy's stepfather, who did that kind of thing all the time. The company was in his name, and Mel would not be remotely connected. "One hundred and fifty acres? What about a six-month option, payable at ten thousand a month? That should be enough to maintain the older couple. We could have a renewable clause, but..." She gave Mel a speculative look. "Perhaps in six months, you and your...er...friend may have come to some...understanding."

Mel was delighted with her suggestion and immediately gave Judy a check, asking her to make the arrangements. "Right away," she urged, "before some other dealer gets to them. And thanks."

"Anything else we can do for you?" Jake asked as she got up to leave.

"No thanks. You've done quite enough." But at the door, she turned back. "Only...if you run across me at some unexpected place..." Like riding a truck, she thought. "Just act as if you don't know me."

She didn't want Tony to see her driving her Jaguar, either, she thought, as she parked the silver sports car in the garage. She wanted to be just what he thought she was...Mel Sands, ordinary working girl. She was even more sure of that when he called to tell her about the exciting option offer his grandparents had received.

"Let's go out to celebrate," he said into the phone. And again they ate spaghetti at Beno's while he told her what she already knew. "They've signed the option, and are preparing to move," he said. "The monthly option is three times as much as the monthly maintenance at the retirement home.

They'll be able to save, and in six months...well, who knows? Anything could happen.''

"Good for you, too, Tony.''

"Yeah. At least I'll be able to market this summer's roses. And I'm saving. Maybe soon I can buy my own place.''

She longed to tell him that the farm was his. But she couldn't. Not until they reached some... understanding.

They were getting closer. Much closer.

She went out to help the elder Costellos make the move. "I can work at my own pace while the boss is away,'' she told Tony who was installing a sprinkling system for somebody. "I'll just borrow Cook's car and drive out.''

Tony's mother was also there to help, and Mel liked her immediately. "Just call me Mom,'' she said, distinguishing herself from the other "Mrs. Costello.'' "That's what all my kids' friends call me.'' She gave Mel a keen look. "You're Tony's friend, aren't you? Thank God,'' she added, as if she was truly glad Tony had a "new friend.'' "That boy's been buried in work. I hope you can help him have some fun.''

Mel hoped so, too. All she had done so far was help him work.

While Tony's mother sorted out and packed Al Costello's clothes, Mel took Mrs. Costello shopping. "I really need to replenish my wardrobe,'' the older woman said. "We'll be dining with the other residents, you know. And my friend, Sarah, who lives there, says they are always going on excursions or getting together for some activity."

Mel could tell she was excited about the move. And no wonder. They would receive the partial care they both needed, and she would be relieved of the responsibilities of cooking and maintaining a very big house, and friends and social activities would brighten the tedium of their days.

What a big difference a little money can make, Mel thought. For some strange reason Dirk came to mind. How badly had he needed that fifty thousand? she wondered. And for what? Had he had an ailing parent or a dream to accomplish? All she really knew about Dirk was how he skied and how he kissed. If he had told her he needed money, she would have told him about the trust fund she was to receive in three years.

Would he have waited?

If he had, she would have married him. And she would never have met Tony. The thought terrified her.

Thank you, Dirk. I hope you enjoyed the fifty thousand, and I hope you loved the hatcheck girl as much as I love Tony, she told the ghost of her past. And exorcised him forever.

During the following three weeks, Mel spent every moment that she possibly could with Tony. The moments without him, she spent thinking about him. He had moved out to the farm so he could see after his grandparents' personal possessions, most of which had been left until after a sale. Cocoa was also left in his care because dogs were not permitted in the retirement home. And, of course, so he could frequently check on his grandparents.

Like his living at the farm was for his family's convenience, rather than his own, Mel thought. But the next thing she learned was that if you wanted to be close to Tony, you had to be close to his family. They were all over each other, got together on every holiday, not to mention about a million birthdays or other minor celebrations. And everybody knew everything about whatever was going on with anyone else in the family. At the Palm Sunday dinner which was held at Tony's parents', Mel was struck by the strong resemblance between the Costello men. She conceded that Tony's father, Joseph Costello, was the most handsome of all, perhaps because of that touch of gray at his temples, so striking against the curly black hair. He also looked as strong and healthy as any of his sons, and considered himself ruler supreme of his entire family. Or at least he tries to be, Mel thought, when she heard him bellow at Don, Frank's oldest son.

"Your father played football. Why are you playing a sissy game like tennis?"

"'Cause I'm good at it," was the complacent answer. "Coach says I have a good chance for a college scholarship."

Joseph Costello sniffed, not impressed. He

glanced at his two offspring who had opted for college. "Marie is up there fiddling around with theatrics when she could be married to Carlo who's already set in his father's roofing business. And Tony's still in school and still ain't got a pot to— Hey, woman! Don't burn me!"

"Sorry, hon," his petite wife answered as she placed two hot biscuits on his plate. "Just wanted you to have these while they're hot. And won't you have a hot one, Mel?" she added, reminding her husband that Tony's "friend" was present, and he should shut up.

He hurriedly buttered his biscuits and began to question the grandfather. How was life at the retirement home?

"It's simply great," the older man answered. "Kinda keeps these old bones moving. Took a trip to a museum the other day, and they've got a bingo game going every Thursday night. I won fifteen dollars last week. Good for Meg, too." He gestured toward his wife who looked ten years younger and as pretty as a peach in that dress they had selected. "First chance she's had to rest in years. Don't you think she's looking great? Yes, sir, I'm glad I signed that option. Best move I ever made."

Mel suppressed a smile. He would never know that his wife had outlined all the arrangements before moving ever crossed his mind. The NOW— National Organization of Women—she thought, could take lessons from the Costello women, who outwardly catered so successfully to their chauvinist men, that they never knew they were being manipulated by the softest of hands.

Mel was absolutely thrilled to be included in these family gatherings. These were practically the only times she saw Tony when he was not working. Besides, his asking her meant that he really liked her, didn't it? And being part of the family was like being part of Tony, wasn't it? Anyway, she enjoyed his family. She enjoyed the camaraderie, the shared meals, the games, the bickering, the teasing. She even enjoyed helping with the meals, the clearing up, and taking turns with the care of Pedro's baby.

There were more babies to care for on the Sunday they gathered at Pedro's for his birthday. Rosalie's sister was there with her two-year-old, and Charlie and his wife from next door brought their baby girl.

"Looks like we're in for an early summer, after all," Joseph Costello declared, mopping his brow.

He was right. The day was pretty hot for April, and many of the guests gathered on the lawn to sit under the shade trees or join in the games. Mel, who, along with Marie, had joined the men for a game of tag football, was feeling pretty sticky.

"Want to go for a swim?" Patsy, who had begun to take Mel for her own particular playmate, pulled on her shirt. "Charlie says we can and he'll come over and watch us. And Marie's coming."

Mel looked at Marie, who nodded. "I'll get a

couple of Rosalie's suits. They should fit...more or less.''

Sid, Frank's youngest boy, and Jerry also joined the girls as they followed Charlie to his pool next door. The sun was warm on their backs, the water refreshing, and the game of water polo, boys against girls, invigorating. Mel was unaware of the passage of time, and was surprised when Tony, looking anxious, came to pull her from the pool. "I've been looking everywhere for you. Come on, they're about to cut the cake."

She knew she looked a mess in the borrowed suit, a bit too big, and her hair dripping wet. It didn't matter. She saw adoration in Tony's dark eyes, reveled in the quiet intimacy of his clasped hand as they walked across the two lawns.

"Stay here," he said. "I'll get cake and ice cream for you."

She watched him walk toward the group gathered around the old-fashioned ice cream freezer, amused and touched that a Costello man was waiting on her. It was supposed to be the other way around, wasn't it? Costello women waited on their men. Was Tony her—?

"Hadn't you better tell him?"

"What?" She spun around. She had been unaware that Charlie was beside her.

"Hadn't you better tell him who you are?" he asked again, his eyes on Tony.

Mel's heart thundered. She had almost forgotten

that this man was the one person here who knew who she was. "I...I will," she stammered. "I did not mean to conceal..." She stopped. She hadn't meant to, but she was glad to be concealed. She liked being...just ordinary, one of them. Her life had always been so orderly, so planned, so apart. So lonely. She looked up at Charlie, willing him to understand. "This is the first time in my life I've been accepted as just me. No trappings."

He smiled. "I know." Then he rubbed his chin, reflecting. "But it won't go away, you know. You can't change who you are any more than I can change the color of my skin. It's part of you."

"I know. And I will tell him," she said.

"The sooner the better," he advised, "I've never seen him this smitten. Well, I see you have your dessert," he said as Tony returned. "I'd better get ours," he added, as he turned to join his wife.

"Thank you." Mel took the ice cream, her eyes on Tony's face, so handsome, so dear to her. Was she as dear to him?

"I've never seen him so smitten," Charlie's words warmed her heart, even as she choked on his bone-chilling advice. "Tell him...the sooner, the better."

I'll tell him tonight, she promised. When we are alone. When he drives me home.

But, later, when she was seated beside him in Pedro's borrowed Mustang, she still procrastinated. This is not the time, she thought. Not while we are in the midst of this back-to-the-city traffic. I'll tell him when we get to the house. When we can face each other and talk.

And perhaps she would have told him then…had he not taken her in his arms and pressed his lips to hers. If she had not been so lost in the intoxicating sweetness of that kiss, so engulfed by compelling erotic sensations that swept through her body and clouded her mind.

If she had not sensed his yearning hunger, heard him whisper, "I'm falling in love with you, Melody Sands."

"Me, too," she whispered back.

She heard his husky laugh. "Crazy, isn't it? I don't want to fall in love. But I can't seem to help myself."

"Me, either."

"You feel it, too?"

She nodded against his shoulder. He pushed back her hair, kissed her temple, traced kisses to her mouth, teased with his tongue. She gave in to the powerful emotions that gripped her, and for a long time there was only touching, feeling.

When he did speak, his voice sounded hoarse, serious. "You feel it, too, this need to be with me always? This longing when we're not together?"

"Yes."

"It's scary, Mel. I've never felt this way before. Hell, I panic every time I bring you home, and watch you go in that house and shut the door. I get a crazy feeling like I might never see you again. What the hell is wrong with me?'' He didn't understand it himself. Why hadn't he taken her back to the farm where they could have given full rein to the passions that gripped both of them?

But he knew why. Because Mel was more than passion. More than a moment of fulfilment.

Mel was commitment. Permanency. Love. He wasn't sure he could live without her.

''Why,'' he asked her now, ''do I feel that I should never let you go? That you are my life, my love. The only one for me?''

''Me, too.''

He smiled. ''Then, what, my little echo, are we going to do about it?''

''I don't know,'' she said. She only knew she wasn't going to spoil this perfect moment with complicated explanations.

CHAPTER SIX

"COULD you get away, just for lunch?" Tony said into the phone. He knew he shouldn't. She said her boss was out of town. Still she seemed to take lots of time off, and he didn't want to jeopardize her job. But, damn, it was like he just had to see her. Gardening job this afternoon, school tonight and... Heck, everybody took off for lunch, didn't they? "Just for lunch," he said again. "I could pick you up. I'm coming into town to deliver some ferns to the Classic."

"You mean we'd have lunch at the Classic?" she asked, sounding more wary than surprised.

"Heck no! Can't afford that. I'll drop the ferns and we'll pick up a couple of burgers, and I'll take you right back. Okay?"

"Okay!"

She sounded as eager to see him as he was to see her, he thought, as he put down the phone. Or maybe she was just eager to get out of that house. It looked like one big empty lonely place to him. And any time he said let's go, she was ready.

He thought about that as he walked toward the barn. He had discovered that she was a private person, a little reluctant to talk about herself. No family evidently, except this father from whom she seemed estranged. But she must have friends. Any woman as likable as Mel, as good-looking… There must be other friends. Other men.

The thought of Mel with any other man made him distinctly uncomfortable. Uncomfortable, hell! He had never felt such a rush of panic. As he climbed to the barn loft, his heart pounded and there was sweat on his brow. He tried to convince himself that he was the only one. The way she welcomed his kisses, responded with such passion. Hell, between her work and the time she spent with him, there wasn't time for anyone else, was there!

But the demon of jealousy persisted. The old fogy she worked for. He was away now. But was there more than an employee/employer relationship there? A live-in secretary? Most unusual. Was she just waiting for his return, marking time until…

He pushed the thought away, ashamed. Mel wasn't the kind of woman who would play with another man while awaiting her lover's return. She was too honest, too forthright.

Too absolutely adorably delightful. He could not get enough of her. He loved the way her blue eyes twinkled, the sound of her soft husky laughter, the feel of her soft beautiful hands. Hands that she didn't mind getting dirty, he thought, remembering how she had labored beside him with all those lilies. She sure was no stranger to work, the way she pitched in with Mom and Rosalie, helped with his grandparents. She fit with the family as easily as she fit into his arms, he thought, grinning as he lifted a heavy potted fern and climbed down from the loft.

He wasn't going to make as much off the ferns as he expected to make off the roses this summer. But he was going to do pretty well with them. A sturdy wild type of fern he had dug from the creek bank before the frost last fall. Now he had several hundred big strong luscious plants he had nurtured in the loft.

"Great. Just the type we need," Link Roberts had said. Link's florist shop had concessions for the supply and care of the plants at several churches and places of business. If his unusual ferns stood up at the Classic, he'd get several more orders, Tony thought as he loaded the truck.

Later, after he had delivered the ferns, and they were sitting on his truck with their hamburgers, he smiled at Mel. "You know something? You're beginning to look as if you belong."

"Belong?" she asked.

"On my truck beside me."

Her smile dazzled him. "Tony Costello, that's the nicest compliment I've ever received. I like belonging beside you on your truck."

She meant it. She really meant it. This most wonderful, most beautiful, most delightful woman he had ever known liked being here with him. She actually looked happy munching on a greasy hamburger with catsup on her chin. A lump rose in his throat. He wanted to take her in his arms right then and there. He wanted to turn the truck around, race back to the farm and make her his.

"Would you like to belong to me?" he whispered, leaning over to lick the catsup from her chin.

"Yes, oh, yes," she answered without hesitation, suddenly still with a French fry halfway to her mouth.

"You'll marry me?"

"Yes, Tony, yes." She put the French fry down, and looked at him like he had just offered her the moon on a silver platter. His heart turned over.

"I love you, Melody Sands."

"And I... Tony, there's something I have to tell you."

Something out of her past that was scaring the hell out of her. Didn't she know how much he loved her? That nothing she had ever done mattered. And he didn't want to hear it. Like he didn't care if the whole world saw him take her in his arms, right here and now. "All I want to know is that you love me," he whispered against her lips.

"I do, I do. I love you, Tony Costello, more than anyone else in the world."

"And that's all that matters to me. When shall we get married?" he asked, still unable to believe that this woman he wanted so much, also wanted him.

"Now."

"Now?" He chuckled. "What about a wedding gown, bridesmaids…?"

"I don't want a wedding. All that planning…people."

He thought of his big family, while she had none. "Anything you say."

"I just want to marry…to be with you."

That was what he wanted, too. He'd been thinking crazy. He didn't want to just turn around and take her to the farm. He wanted her permanently, legally. He was scheduled for that gardening job in just one hour. A man had to work. But if they were married…after work, or school, she would always be there waiting for him. "Come on," he said. "City hall's just around the corner. We at least have time to get a license."

It was Veronica Landsen's habit to make frequent stops at city hall's licensing bureau. Sometimes who was applying to marry whom made an interesting news item, sometimes even a scoop. Today, Veronica was only here to renew the license of her prize poodle. However, she found herself intrigued by the couple next to her who were third in line for a marriage license. She didn't know why. They were a striking couple, but quite ordinary. Nobody special.

Definitely in love, she thought, watching them. But of course that was always the way…when one was on the way to the marriage altar. Veronica, who had just ended her third try, gave a bitter sigh. Men! They come on with all that sweetness and love you. It was later that you learned it was crap.

This one was a handsome hunk, all right. Looked like a movie star, even in those worn jeans and pullover. But she was sure she had never seen him before. Besides, those calloused hands that kept fingering the girl's red hair had certainly seen plenty of manual labor.

That hair now... A most unusual golden red that somehow touched a memory. Her face seemed familiar, too. Veronica, veteran reporter, did not often forget a face.

Her interest perked. Something different about her. She could swear that sleeveless shirt was pure silk, the jeans too perfect a fit, those loafers a soft kidskin. She could almost swear it.

"Melody Costello," she heard the man say when they were second in line. "I like it. More euphonious than Melody Sands, don't you think?"

Veronica missed the woman's answer as memory catapulted through her mind. Melody. A most unusual name. Melody. Melody Sands. Now her mind raced backward. Some years back...wasn't there some scandal about a Sands heiress who had eloped with some undesirable somebody. She'd get back to the *Tribune* and do some research.

But not until she saw the couple depart. Saw them get into a truck that held what seemed to be gardening equipment and plants.

* * *

"Tony, I want to tell you something," Melody said when they got back into the truck.

"Later, sweetheart," he said. "Things are happening so fast. We need to plan. Are you sure you want to get married tomorrow?" When they had learned that there was only a twenty-four-hour waiting period, she seemed pleased and urged, "Let's do it tomorrow, Tony. Let's don't wait."

She had seemed so anxious that he couldn't even laugh when he teased, "Don't worry, sweet. I'm not going anywhere."

She hadn't laughed, either. "I know. I just don't want to wait...to have to explain, tell people. Please?"

"Of course, sweetheart. I'm as anxious as you. And I don't want a lot of fuss, either." So they had arranged for a civil ceremony in the clerk's office at one-thirty the next day.

But now, as he sat in the truck, anxious to get her back home, and get to his job—he was already late—he found himself hard put to face the mammoth decision they had just made.

"At least we have a place to live. For six months anyway," he said, explaining certain realities to her as much as to himself. By that time, with the roses and ferns, and the summer jobs he had lined up, he would have enough to rent a fairly decent apartment. "You can keep working if you want to. But I'd rather you didn't," he added. "I know you'll have to give notice. We'll talk about it later."

"Tony, I have to tell—"

"Pedro!" he exclaimed. "I'll have to tell him. I'd like him to stand with us."

"Of course. And Rosalie. They can be our witnesses. But, Tony—"

"Here we are. I gotta go, hon. I'll have to call Pedro and see if he can arrange to get off. Later," he said, as he lifted her down and kissed her.

She watched him drive away, her heart in her mouth.

She hadn't told him.

I tried to. But every time I started, he stopped me.

You stopped yourself. You didn't want to tell him.

Hot waves of guilt gushed through her. That was true. She hadn't wanted anything to spoil the moment. She had been stunned, but so absolutely deliriously bowled over with happiness when Tony asked her to marry him...

That you would have married him right then and there if you could have.

Well, yes. She wanted it over before anything could stop them.

Like your father arriving two days from now?

I'm not under his control anymore. He couldn't stop me.

Could stop your little farce, couldn't he? Poor little working girl...

She was suddenly angry. What, for Pete's sake,

was wrong with being rich! She'd been acting like she had the plague or something. Tony loved her, not her money. What a warm, delicious feeling that gave her. And her money wouldn't interfere with their life. It would just make things easier. She could tell, right after they got the license, that Tony was worried...about where and how they were going to live.

Well, now he would know he wouldn't have to worry. Things would be easier. He wouldn't have to continue with all those small jobs that took time away from his nursery and his school. He could build his greenhouses, hire more men, concentrate on school. Money would be a filler. Her wedding gift to him.

She went into the house, happy and at peace. After tomorrow, there would be no secrets between them.

"Do you, Anthony Costello, take this woman to be your lawful wedded wife?" the Justice of the Peace intoned.

"I do." Tony answered all the questions in a strong vigorous voice, meaning every word. He wanted it to be a memorable day for Mel, and he had planned carefully. At least Rosalie, who seemed even more excited than he, had planned.

"Bad luck for you to see her before the ceremony," she had said. "So we'll pick her up in the station wagon, and you can take the Mustang. Can't drive off in a truck with your new bride. And I'll make reservations for the four of us. A late lunch at the Classic, mine and Pedro's treat.''

He was glad she had made such plans. It would be a real celebration, champagne, toasts, and all. Pregnant as she was, Rosalie looked very pretty in that pale pink dress.

But no one was as beautiful as his Mel. He was glad she was wearing white. A soft, sheer bride's white that fell freely from her shoulders to ripple about her knees. A tiny white orchid was tucked in her gorgeous red hair that was piled upon her head in a way that made her lovely features more enchanting than ever.

He slipped the simple gold band upon her finger, loving her with every fiber of his being, vowing that he would always keep her happy.

''I pronounce you man and wife,'' the Justice said.

It was over. He kissed his bride, happier than he had ever been in his life. Then the four of them went wild, hugging and kissing each other, laughing as they emerged from the courthouse.

Something must have happened, he thought, as they started down the steps. Such a big crowd, TV cameras and all.

Before he had a chance to take it in, to wonder, he felt the flash of a photographer's bulb, and a mike was thrust into his face.

''Mr. Costello, how does it feel to be married to an heiress?''

CHAPTER SEVEN

MORE blinding flashes. More questions. Thick and fast. "What are your plans? Where are you going for a honeymoon? Where did you meet?" But the one question that thundered through his mind was, "How does it feel to be married to an heiress?"

It felt like being doused with a bucket of ice water in midwinter. Like he wanted to bash somebody. Or cry. Like he wanted to get the hell away from here.

He tried to push his way through the crowd. He kept muttering, "No comment. No comment."

Wasn't that what you said when you were caught looking like a fool? When someone had lied to you? Someone you trusted. When someone got you trapped like a fox in front of a bunch of news hounds. He kept pushing, kept muttering, "No comment. Pardon. Excuse me, please." He saw Pedro, who looked confused, spirit Rosalie safely away, thank God. But Rosalie, looking worried, was trying to say something, was reaching out...

That was when he turned to see Mel. She was backed up against the courthouse wall, barricaded by a barrage of reporters, battered by questions.

One blond woman was asking, "Why do these types of men appeal to you?"

It hit him like a hot brick. *These types of men.* What the hell did that mean?

Mel kept her mouth shut tight. But the woman was persistent. "Have you forgotten Dirk Johanson? What will your father do now?"

Mel shook her head and backed against the wall, trying to get away. Her tortured face sent blinding rage surging through him. He moved swiftly, almost knocking a man down. "Get the hell out of my way."

The crowd was no match for his fury. Within minutes he had bolted through, picked Mel up and escaped with her to the car. He squealed out of the parking lot, caring little whom or what he hit.

"Slow down, Tony. You might hurt someone."

He lifted his foot from the gas pedal. He didn't want to hurt anyone.

"Tony…"

"Shut up." He didn't want to hurt Mel. He just wanted her out of the car. Out of his life.

"Tony, let me explain."

"No need. I understand. And now that you've had your little fling, you can—"

"It's not a fling! We're married."

"Not for long." An annulment would be easy.

"What…what do you mean?" The question came out in a little squeak. "Where are you taking me?"

"Home to Daddy." He had learned enough from the questions to know that her "estranged" father was rich and powerful. That he spent his money like crazy to protect her from predators. Well, he was no damn predator, and he sure as hell didn't like looking like one! In front of the whole damn world, for Pete's sake!

"Tony, I'm not going home. I'm going with you."

"You're not going with me."

"If you take me home, I won't get out of the car."

"Oh, I think you will. I'm bigger than you."

But when he turned into Clayborn Drive and saw the paneled TV trucks, he hesitated.

"Go on, put me out," Mel taunted, an edge to her voice. "Throw me to the wolves."

"Don't tempt me." But he swiftly cut into a side street. He could just take her to some hotel. But there was no escape in the city, and he couldn't bring himself to "throw her to the wolves."

Neither of them spoke on that long drive to the farm. Mel found herself praying harder than she had ever prayed in her life. Please God, make him listen, understand. Everything had been so perfect, so beautiful, so loving. She hadn't meant for it to come to this. How had it happened? Her wedding gift had blown up in her face. She had meant it for a surprise. But not like this. Not a humiliation.

Still, it wasn't her fault. Could she help it if there

were nosy reporters who always found out everything there was to know about anybody, and splashed it all over the whole world so everybody would know!

Okay. What was it for them to know, for Pete's sake? So she was rich. Lots of people were rich. It's not a disease.

Tony had no right to act like she had been caught in some horrible scandal. Like she was so besmirched, he wouldn't dare touch her with his lily-white hands.

By the time they reached the farm, she was as angry as he. When he stormed into the house, she followed.

"Why exactly are you so mad?" she asked, reaching down to pet Cocoa who was jumping on her white sandals, scratching at her bare legs.

His eyes bored into hers as if she was stupid to ask such a dumb question. He flung his jacket to the couch, took off his tie and rolled up his sleeves before answering. Slowly and deliberately. "You lied to me."

"I did not lie. You assumed."

"Bull!" He turned his back on her and went into the kitchen.

She followed, watched him reach into the cabinet for dog food to pour into Cocoa's dish.

"You know you did, Tony." She walked to the sink and filled the dog's bowl with fresh water.

"That very first morning when I brought that coffee to you, you assumed I was the maid or something."

"You sure as hell helped me with the assumption."

"I never lied."

"Oh?" He leaned against the counter and raised an eyebrow. "How about 'I'm a secretary'?"

"I never said that. You asked me what I did at that house and I told you I took care of papers for the man of the house. And I do...sometimes."

"Look, let's not nitpick around the truth you've been hiding for the past two months! The man of the house! Your father. One of the small details you forgot to mention." He gave her a cutting look and strode back into the living room.

"Because of your stupid bias," she screamed, following him. "Do you know what you are, Tony Costello? You are a stupid, arrogant, supercilious bigot!"

He shot her a surprised look. "I am not a bigot."

"Oh, yes, you are. A bigot is someone who despises someone else because they're not the same color, class, creed, or whatever that he is. You despise me because I'm rich and you're not."

"I don't despise you. I just don't like being lied to."

"Stop saying that!"

"It's not what I say. The fact is—"

"Okay, have it your way! I lied. So now you know the truth."

"And the truth makes a difference."

"Why?"

"You're out of my class, lady."

"We were pretty damn chummy when you didn't know I was rich. If all you were interested in was money, why didn't you investigate my financial situation a long time ago?"

"Oh, Mel, you know I don't care about the money."

"You don't? Then pray tell me, what is the problem?"

"Okay, okay." He ran a hand through his hair. "I don't... I... Oh, hell, maybe it does make a difference."

"How so? I haven't changed, have I?"

"Not you. Circumstance. Before...it was like, well, we were more on an equal basis. Don't you see?"

"No, I don't see. I bet if it were the other way around, money wouldn't make a difference."

"What do you mean?"

"I mean if you had it and I didn't, you bigoted son of a..." She stopped, her hand over her mouth. "No. I don't mean that. I won't say a word against your sweet mother. She's a wonderful, caring, unselfish, giving woman. She can't help it that she's married to a loud-mouthed, dogmatic chauvinist, and has spawned three of same."

He frowned. "What are you talking about?"

"I'm talking about your father who tries to be a

dictator. He'd like to stifle your sister who wants to have a fling at acting while she's young and pretty enough to do it. He wants her to settle down and marry that boy next door and have babies like Rosalie. And Marie's only eighteen! And I'm talking about your brother Frank who won't let his wife take a job. Sarah told me herself that she's going stir crazy in that big house now that the boys are in their teens and don't need her as much, and they could sure use extra money for college.''

"So!" Tony broke in when she paused for breath. "You resent the fact that Costello men want to support their families."

"I resent that they want to be in control. That they'd like to keep their women under their thumb like some crawling worm."

"That's not true!"

"Yes, it is. And you're the same worm-squashing type, Tony Costello. If you had the money and I didn't. If you were in control, every-thing between us would be all hunky-dory, wouldn't it?"

Tony's face looked like a thundercloud. "But you've got the money, and you're in control, huh? You plan to go on in your pampered, spoiled, having-everything-your-own-way, huh? Well, not this time. We're ending this facade. And right now, I've got work to do." He started toward the door.

"Tony, wait! I didn't mean—"

He turned back. "You can stay here tonight.

Take the big bedroom. I'll sleep in my old room. Alone! Nothing will interfere with a quick annulment.''

"Tony..."

"We've talked enough. No need to spoil things more than they already are." The screen door slammed behind him.

"I didn't mean it, I didn't mean it," she whispered to herself. She had just been so mad! Cook always said her redheaded temper would get her into trouble.

Cook. She had promised to bring Tony by after the wedding. And now...she would be alone in that house, hounded by reporters. She picked up the phone.

"Don't worry about me, honey," came Cook's reassuring voice. "It's you they're after. Are you all right?"

"Yes." She would never be all right again.

"And your young man? Is he—"

"Okay," she lied. Well, he was, wasn't he? Going on with his stupid work. He didn't care about her.

"I guess you know you're all over the news. They're dragging up all that old stuff about that Swedish guy."

She didn't want to hear it. She got off the phone as quickly as she could. She felt so tired. She climbed the stairs and threw herself across the big bed that was to have been her wedding bed. She had never felt so alone in life.

The phone on the bedside table rang, startling her.

It was Rosalie. "Oh, Mel, I'm so sorry. Are you all right?"

"Yes."

"No, you're not. Tony's mad, isn't he?"

"Yes." A sob caught in her throat. She had made it worse by getting mad herself.

"Yeah. I knew he would be. And when he sees the news... Where is he?"

"Out working."

"That mad, huh?"

"Oh, Rosalie, we had a big fight. Shouting and calling names." The tears were flowing freely now and she brushed them away with her fist. "I don't know what to do. Tony's so mad."

"He'll get over it."

"You think so?"

"Sure. He's crazy about you."

He's crazy about you, crazy about you. The words sang in her ear, warmed her heart. She tried to hope.

"And you're the best thing that's happened to him, Mel. Just hang in there until he simmers down."

"Oh, Rosalie, I don't think he will. He's so mad."

"Well, it was a shock, you know. Right in his

face. He had to blow off some steam. That's the way he is. Pedro, too. When something upsets them, they come on like a thunderstorm. But underneath, they're soft as cotton. Just cuddle up and love him. He'll come 'round.''

How could she cuddle up when he wouldn't allow her near him? Mel wondered as she put the phone down. Still, she was comforted by Rosalie's call. Rosalie talked to her like…well, just woman to woman. Not one word about ''You're rich, and why didn't you tell us?'' Just… ''You're my friend and this is what I think you ought to do.''

Somehow the call put a bit of spunk in her. Enough, anyway, to get to her feet, take the pins from her hair. She shook her hair loose, laid the tiny orchid on the dresser…beside the roses. Roses. Not the perfect, staid, stiff long-stem roses like the ones Adrian always sent. These were ordinary, kinda old-fashioned, real rose-colored roses, some tiny buds and some in the glory of full bloom. Their sweet fragrance filled the room. She bent to touch one, and caught another odor. A faint pine scent, rather refreshing. Furniture polish.

Mel ran a finger over the spotless dresser, looked around the room. Everything in place, clean and fresh.

Tony. He had worked all yesterday afternoon. He had come home late. Cleaned, polished, prepared for her.

He would have brought in the roses this morning.

So they would be there. For her. On her wedding night.

Even today, when everything blew up in his face, he thought first of her. It was Tony who had picked her up and rescued her from those reporters.

Even though he was mad at her. And he had a right to be mad. She had lied to him. All along. Because she was scared that if he knew she was rich, she would lose him. She knew about the Costello men.

She thought about that. As mad as Tony was with her, he had protected her. Because he couldn't help being what he was...loving, protective, supportive.

Like all the Costello men. The men she had called dogmatic, dictatorial chauvinists. Well, so they were, weren't they? So protective that they could smother you.

Only they didn't. She thought about that, too. Thought about Tony's grandmother arranging everything before moving had even occurred to her husband. Thought of Marie, waiting on her father, kissing his cheek, and going on doing what he didn't want her to do. Tony's mother had her husband wrapped around her finger with just her sweet soft words. And she bet Sarah would talk Frank into letting her take a job. She was already brushing up on her typing.

Maybe, Mel thought, *she* should take a lesson from the Costello women.

It was dark by the time she heard Tony return to

the house. He was being very quiet, but she heard him come up the stairs. Heard the shower running. Heard him retire to the little room that had always been his.

She got off the bed. Slipped out of the room, walked down the darkened hall on bare feet.

She stood in his doorway, and took a deep breath. "Tony, I love you. Doesn't that count?"

CHAPTER EIGHT

HER words came in a soft whisper, but his ears captured the music. "I love you, Tony." A soothing balm, healing a hurt that three hours of digging had failed to erase.

She stood in the doorway. Apart. A ghost that might fade away.

Panic seized him. He rushed to take her in his arms, to hold her there forever. "Stay with me, Mel. Don't leave me."

"I won't, Tony. Not ever. I love you."

Then it came out together and all at once. Words tumbling over words, sentences, jumbled, broken and incomplete. Explanations, apologies, reassurance. "Sorry...didn't mean...only you...nothing else matters...I love you...love you...love you."

And then there were no words. Only a rush of sweet exhilarating feeling, as pulses quickened and hearts pounded with erotic yearnings too deep and powerful to be denied.

Tony picked her up, and stepped over his discarded clothes to get to his narrow bed.

She shook her head against his chest. "No."

"No! Good God, Mel, I can't—"

"Not here. In there with my roses," she said, her lips against the throbbing pulse at his throat.

She would always remember. The scent of roses, the rapturous joy, the magic of happy fulfilment as she became one with Tony Costello on their wedding night.

She awoke to the sound of birds chirping in the trees outside, early morning sun warm on her face, a soft breeze filtering through the curtains, stirring the rose-scented air.

Tony's lips against her ear. "Are you happy, Mrs. Costello?"

"Yes! Oh, yes! Happier than I've ever been in my entire life!"

"I promise to keep you happy..."

"I know." She ran a finger across his mouth, touched that crooked tooth. Smiled as she thought of fresh sheets, furniture polish, roses. "Tony, I loved the roses. They made me feel so special."

He kissed her. "Because they tell you of my love. The rose, my sweet, is the flower of romance."

"Oh?"

"Sure. Didn't you know that? Cleopatra walked through a bed of rose petals to receive Mark Anthony. Medieval ladies bathed in rose water and scattered rose petals among the linens to entice their men."

Mel sat up, ran a hand along the sheets, searching. "Where are the petals you should have put here to entice me?"

"Touché!" He laughed as he pulled her back into his arms. "No need. I knew that old rose fragrance would get you, even from way over there."

"*Old* rose?" She snuggled against him. "Different from the modern hybrids, huh?"

"Most roses are hybrids of one kind or another. It is said that while Napoleon was waging war with all those countries, his Josephine was trading cuttings with enemy horticulturists to amass the vast and most imperial rose collection in history."

"Oh, Tony, that's so touching...but so sad. Men dying while she peacefully planted roses."

"Regrettably, roses have a history of violence, too. Remember the Wars of the Roses?"

"Huh?"

"Between the House of York with the white rose, and the House of Lancaster with the red?"

She sat up again. "Tony Costello, how come you know so much that I don't?"

He chuckled. "Just about flowers, love. Because I grow them. And roses are my specialty. I want to know all about them, history and all."

"I see." She studied him, thinking of his grandmother. "He got out those books, studied." He not only worked hard, he... "You like to know every detail of any project you undertake, don't you?"

"Only when it's important. You know that plot set off from the other rose beds?"

"Yes."

"Well, I'm doing a little grafting. I'm working on developing a rose patent of my own."

"Rose patent?"

He told her more that she didn't know. How different varieties were developed, and sometimes patented. He told her about his experimental grafting in technical terms she didn't understand, what might happen and how it might look. She couldn't quite comprehend, but she was fascinated. This was her Tony, enthusiastic, determined, talking about his plans, his dreams. Just as he had that first night at the spaghetti house.

"If things work out, I plan to show it at the American Horticultural Science Conference in the early fall. It might be ready, really in bloom by then." He frowned. "I've been thinking I ought to build a shelter of some kind. Sure don't want it crushed by one of our thunderstorms."

If he had a greenhouse, she thought. She could... She put her hand over her mouth to stifle the thought. This was *his* dream. The pleasure was in working for it. People didn't want their dreams handed to them on a silver platter.

She thought of something else. This morning they had talked about anything but the one thing that had almost torn them apart. Her money.

Well, she vowed, it wouldn't tear them apart and Tony would have his dream.

"That's absolutely fascinating," she said. "It

PLAY TIC-TAC-TOE

FOR FREE BOOKS AND A GREAT FREE GIFT!

Use this sticker to **PLAY TIC-TAC-TOE**. See instructions inside!

THERE'S NO COST•NO OBLIGATION!

Get **2** books and a fabulous mystery gift! **ABSOLUTELY FREE!**

Turn the page to play!

Play **TIC-TAC-TOE** and get **FREE GIFTS!**

HOW TO PLAY:

1. Play the tic-tac-toe scratch-off game at the right for your FREE BOOKS and FREE GIFT!

2. Send back this card and you'll receive TWO brand-new Harlequin Romance® novels. These books have a cover price of $3.50 each, but they are yours to keep absolutely free.

3. There's no catch. You're under no obligation to buy anything. We charge nothing — ZERO — for your first shipment. And you don't have to make any minimum number of purchases — not even one!

4. The fact is, thousands of readers enjoy receiving books by mail from the Harlequin Reader Service® months before they're available in stores. They like the convenience of home delivery, and they love our discount prices!

5. We hope that after receiving your free books you'll want to remain a subscriber. But the choice is yours — to continue or cancel, any time at all! So why not take us up on our invitation, with no risk of any kind. You'll be glad you did!

YOURS **FREE**
A FABULOUS **MYSTERY GIFT!**

**We can't tell you what it is…
but we're sure you'll like it!**

A FREE GIFT—
just for playing

TIC-TAC-TOE!

First, scratch the gold boxes on the tic-tac-toe board. Then remove the "X" sticker from the front and affix it so that you get three X's in a row. This means you can get TWO FREE Harlequin Romance® novels and a **FREE MYSTERY GIFT!**

PLAY TIC-TAC-TOE

YES! Please send me all the gifts for which I qualify. I understand that I am under no obligation to purchase any books, as explained on the back of this card.

(U-H-R-08/98)   **116 HDL CH5Y**

Name
_____
(PLEASE PRINT CLEARLY)

Address _____ Apt.#_____

City _____ State _____ Zip _____

The Harlequin Reader Service® — Here's how it works:

Accepting free books places you under no obligation to buy anything. You may keep the books and gift and return the shipping statement marked "cancel." If you do not cancel, about a month later we'll send you 6 additional novels and bill you just $2.90 each, plus 25¢ delivery per book and applicable sales tax, if any.* That's the complete price — and compared to cover prices of $3.50 each — quite a bargain! You may cancel at any time, but if you choose to continue, every month we'll send you 6 more books, which you may either purchase at the discount price...or return to us and cancel your subscription.

*Terms and prices subject to change without notice. Sales tax applicable in N.Y.

If offer card is missing write to: Harlequin Reader Service, 3010 Walden Ave., P.O. Box 1867, Buffalo NY 14240-1867

BUSINESS REPLY MAIL
FIRST-CLASS MAIL   PERMIT NO. 717   BUFFALO, NY

POSTAGE WILL BE PAID BY ADDRESSEE

HARLEQUIN READER SERVICE
3010 WALDEN AVE
PO BOX 1867
BUFFALO NY 14240-9952

NO POSTAGE
NECESSARY
IF MAILED
IN THE
UNITED STATES

sounds like it will be a beautiful rose, that deep rose fading into lavender.''

"Well, if it turns out like I plan. And if I can protect it.''

"Screens. Couldn't we build some screens around it, and maybe over the top?''

"We?" He smiled at her. "You know something, Mel? The first thing I noticed about you...no, the second, after your gorgeous hair. Your hands.'' He took her left hand in his, touched the little wedding band, kissed her palm, sending shivers of delight through her. "I want them to stay soft and beautiful.''

"I'll wear gloves,'' she said, trying to think. How could she put it so it wouldn't be a lie? "Tony, we need to talk.''

"I know.'' But she could tell he was reluctant.

"I'm just an heiress, you know. Dad's money belongs to him.'' That much was true. "I do have some money. Not much,'' she said, her fingers crossed behind her. "Not enough to make a difference.'' Nothing could make a difference in their love.

"I see,'' he said. "What you're telling me is that the bulk of your fortune is still in your father's hands and he's not likely to look with favor upon this union. That bothers you?''

"Yes. I mean no! I mean, no, it doesn't bother me. But yes, he might not like it.'' Maybe, she thought, that would be a way. If Dad raised hell like he did about Dirk...

"Mel..." Tony looked as if he had suddenly thought of something that worried him. "Who is Dirk Johanson?"

"Nobody. At least... Oh, Tony I was young and foolish and I didn't know what real love was." She told him then. All of it. He held her close while she talked, as if to protect her from the pain she had suffered so long ago. "But you know something, Tony? I'm glad. If Dirk hadn't deserted, I would never have met you, married you. I couldn't live without you, Tony," she said, hugging him to her.

He rumpled her hair, kissed her temple. "Nor can I live without you, sweet. But...could you live without money? Your Dad..."

"Yes, Tony, I could. I'd like to." Here, thank God, was the way out. "I hope Dad does raise hell, makes threats, disinherits me. I don't care. I'd like it. Even if he didn't, I'd like to prove that I could live without all that money. Don't you see? Tony, couldn't we pretend it doesn't exist and just go on living as we planned before you ever knew about it? I know I didn't tell you, and I'm sorry. But couldn't we, Tony? Couldn't we? It would prove something to me as well as to Dad."

"I don't know. You've always had money. It won't be easy." He sounded skeptical, but she could tell he was beginning to look relieved. "Are you sure this is what you want to do?"

"Yes. Other women do it. I could, too. I want to prove it to myself as well as to Dad." And I want you to accomplish your dream all on your own, she thought. "Please, Tony. We won't even touch the little I have. Please?"

He looked down at her hands. "Well...if you promise to wear gloves."

CHAPTER NINE

IN THE kitchen three mornings later, Mel filled the pot with cold water, carefully measured out coffee, added a dash of salt just as Jake had taught her. She wasn't sure about the coffee, but, luckily, this was the same kind of pot as in the galley of Jake's boat. She hummed as she started the bacon and set the little breakfast table with the prettiest matching dishes in the cabinet. She wondered if it would be all right to discard the mismatched ones.

The past two days had been heavenly. They had stayed at the farm, undisturbed. The reporters hadn't found them, or hadn't wanted to. They had had their scoop, and moved on to fresher, more spectacular news. Leaving them miraculously alone.

Mel smiled, remembering. That first day they had been totally involved with each other. They had made love, talked, snacked on what was available, talked…made love.

The second day… Well, she knew she couldn't keep him from work forever. He had rescheduled his jobs in town, but said he couldn't let things at the farm go. So they got up early. She had fixed him a proper breakfast, and while it was still cool,

100

had walked with him down to the creek where he dug up more of those ferns he said might bring in more money than the roses. It was lovely there on the shady bank of the creek, and she itched to help, to feel that damp earth on her fingers. But he wouldn't let her. He had this thing about her hands. She was going to have to do something about that. Hadn't she read somewhere that working with your hands in the soil was therapeutic? It sure did something for Tony...so strong, graceful, precise. She loved to watch him work, just as she had that very first day.

"Good morning, love." Tony's arms were around her, his lips nuzzling the back of her neck.

She leaned closer. "Oh, Tony, do you have to go to work today?" In town, where she couldn't be beside him.

"Afraid so, sweet. Olsen's depending on me, and I'm two days' late already. But I will return," he promised in a soft suggestive whisper that teased her ear.

"Doesn't your grandmother have a cookbook somewhere?" she asked when they were seated at breakfast.

"I don't know. I never saw her use one."

"Well, I need one." Envy was fast giving way to rage at those women who instinctively knew how to do whatever they had to do.

"You're doing fine, honey. Spoiling me already. Before this, I worked all morning on an empty stomach. Never had breakfast till noon, and not then unless I was near some fast-food joint.''

''Thank you for the kind words, sir. But we can't live on bacon and eggs.'' Which was all she had learned to cook on Jake's boat. The dinner she had tried to fix last evening while he was working in his roses was a disaster.

His eyes twinkled and she knew he was remembering. ''Why not? I like bacon and eggs. I…'' He stopped. They both heard it. A car coming up the lane.

They both stood and rushed down the hall toward the front.

The black chauffeur-driven limousine came to a stop. The reporters hadn't come, but her father had. He got out of the car, a tall, formidable figure in his tailored business suit, the fighting uniform of his trade…a mover and a shaker in the powerful world of finance. Ignoring Cocoa's vicious barks, he mounted the steps, a threatening figure.

Mel's heart sank. He was going to spoil everything!

Tony pushed open the screen door. ''Good morning, sir. Won't you come in?''

Samuel Sands stepped in, glared at Tony. ''Costello?''

''Right. Tony Costello. And you, I take it, are Mel's father. Glad to meet you, sir.'' Tony extended his hand.

Mel glanced at her father. He stared at the out-

stretched hand, finally shook it, as nonplussed as
she to find Tony taking the initiative. He tried to
get it back, and snapped out a taking-charge com-
mand. "Costello, I came here for some straight
talk."

"Of course. Come join us. We're just having coffee," Tony said, leading the way to the kitchen.

Samuel Sands followed, but when they reached
what had been a pleasant breakfast scene, he turned
his wrath on his daughter. "I see that you, as usual,
have managed to make a spectacle of yourself."

His disapproval always made her cower. She
found herself stuttering. "I...I..."

"Not her fault, sir. We didn't invite the press."
Tony stepped between them, laid a protective arm
lightly on her shoulder. "Get your father a cup of
coffee, hon." He pulled out a chair. "Sit here, sir.
Would you like toast? Breakfast?"

Sands sat down, but shook his head, seeming, for
the moment, speechless.

Tony also sat, and took up his fork to finish his
interrupted breakfast. Looking as much at ease as
he did transplanting a rosebush, he inquired, "You
wish to talk, sir?"

"Damn right! You are aware that my daughter
is a very rich woman."

"He isn't...wasn't..." Mel's hand shook, and
the cup clattered against the saucer that she set before her father. "He didn't know who I was. He
thought I worked at your...our house. It wasn't un-

til after we were married, and those awful reporters showed up that he found out.''

"Bull! Opportunists know when to keep quiet.''

"Dad!'' Mel glanced at Tony who, as far as she could tell, actually seemed amused. "He didn't know. He didn't. He was as mad as fire when he found out. He—''

"Mel, you don't need to defend me.''

"Yes, I do. I won't have him thinking you're a fortune hunter.'' She looked down at her father, eyes blazing. "We don't need your money. We're going to live on what we have.''

"What *you* have, huh? I see,'' he said, and she wondered if Tony caught the sarcasm. "You can do as you damn well please, huh? Now that you're past twenty-one and have—''

"Now that I have Tony,'' she broke in. "We can live on what he earns. We don't need any more.'' Her eyes bored into her father's, willing him, begging him. If he mentioned her trust fund...

His eyes reflected surprise, disbelief. Irony. "Quite independent all of a sudden, aren't you? Didn't learn anything from those soup kitchens in Vegas, did you? Well, let me tell—''

Tony's chair flew back, and he was on his feet. "Don't badger my wife!''

Sands, halted in midsentence, stared up at him. Then he, too, stood, poised for battle. "Listen, you. She's my daughter and I can—''

"Dad!" Mel pulled on his sleeve, turned pleading eyes toward her husband. "Tony, please..."

Tony's gentle, but firm hand pressed her back into her chair. "Finish your breakfast, sweetheart." Then he turned to her father. "It's not your daughter. It's me that concerns you, isn't it, sir? You wanted straight talk. Well, let's get something straight. I'm not on welfare, and I'm not looking for a handout. I've been taking care of myself for several years now, and I can take care of my wife."

Sands snorted and shot a skeptical glance around the kitchen. "My daughter is accustomed to a certain style of life that I seriously doubt you can provide."

"Right. I understand your concern. It won't be easy for her." The flicker of doubt in his voice cut her to the quick.

She ran to his side. "It will be easy, Tony. As long as I am with you."

Tony slipped an arm around her. "Her decision, sir."

Sands mouth twisted. "And now that she is over twenty-one and has—"

"I have promised to live on what Tony earns, damn it!" She stabbed him with her eyes, daring him to expose her trust fund! She watched him, seeing the doubt, the suspicion. But she saw something else, too...a faint glimmer of respect.

He shrugged. "Well, it's your bed! Get me another cup of coffee. This is cold."

Mel rushed to take his cup, her eyes signaling "thank you." She breathed a sigh of relief as she refilled the cup. She knew her father. This wasn't the end. He would have his bloodhounds examine every inch of Tony's life.

And everything he finds will be good, she thought, feeling a strong glow of pride.

Tony would have his dream...of his own making. She would make sure of that.

Still, apprehension persisted. How long could she play that option game? What if the area was re-zoned, and someone else offered to buy?

Well, she would just have to cross that bridge when she got to it.

Cooking was her main concern. Any man who worked as hard as Tony ought to come in to a delicious body-building dinner.

But he was saddled with a wife who could hardly boil water.

She could consult Cook. That brought forth a giggle. Cook did not quite live up to her name. Now, if Lorenza, the chef her father maintained at their house in Palm Springs was nearby...

Shucks! Anybody who could read could cook.

Not like Rosalie.

Rosalie! Of course. Where had her mind gone? Why was she thinking of fancy chefs when Rosalie, with her never-measured, mouth-watering Southern cooking, was available. Either by phone or car, now that Mel had the use of Grandfather Costello's old Ford. He didn't drive anymore and his wife never had.

Rosalie said she liked having her, that she was a big help with the kids. Especially Buddy, with his constant activity and toilet training.

"You must get bored," Rosalie said one day as she showed her how to fold the dough around the fresh peaches in the cobbler they were making. "I know you must be accustomed to an active social life. Tony spends so much time in town working, and you're out there on the farm by yourself. Must drive you up the wall!"

"No. Never." She loved being at the farm…so serene and quiet with Tony's summer crop of flowers blooming all around her. Just thinking about Tony kept her from ever being bored. To be in his arms the whole long night was worth all the waiting. "Besides," she said, "there's so much to do." Mostly cleaning and clearing out, she thought.

Mrs. Costello said it was all right to discard those mismatched dishes. "Lots of other junk you could throw out," she had added. "I'd like to have a hand in it. Al made me save everything."

So one day she had brought his grandmother out to the farm, and they had had a ball. Tossing out old papers and magazines, discarded clothing, odds and ends that did nothing but clutter. They packed objects useful to be given to Goodwill, and carefully stored family treasures.

Family treasures...like pictures of Tony as a baby and in his teens that touched Mel's heart, and brought him closer. Someday she would make an album. Perhaps she could collect more from his mother.

Clearing it of clutter seemed to make more space in the old house. Except in that tiny bathroom with its squeaky pipes and the wall crumbling above the bathtub. Sharing a bath was difficult enough. Mel had always had her own private bathroom, much larger than their present bedroom. She found it hard to maneuver in this one among Tony's shaving things, toothbrush, and the toothpaste which he always left open. She solved some of this by purchasing a stand, easily mounted over the toilet stool, which afforded extra towel racks and a cabinet for her cosmetics.

She wished she could do more. Like tear out this bathroom and replace it.

More. Like refurbish the powder room downstairs. Tear out some walls upstairs to make a big master bedroom with two big baths and their own private deck.

She could do this. Even more. Easily. Just call in a decorator and a contractor, sit back and wait.

But...a promise was a promise. And keeping her promise to Tony created money problems. Not just decorating money.

Grocery money. Oh, there was always money in the joint checking account Tony had opened, and added to every week. Well, at least every other week, usually whenever Link Roberts, the florist who now bought cut flowers as well as ferns, paid him. But people were sometimes late paying, and Tony always needed money in his business account...for things like fertilizer, plant food, pots, new equipment, or something for the truck. He really needed to hire some help, now that it was summer and he had flowers growing all over the place. She hated to see him come home from town to work with his plants every evening. If he could hire a man...

He wouldn't. She knew he was counting every penny, preparing for the day someone would take up that option, and he would have to move his business. He never attended summer classes, but now he thought he might stay out of school for one year. "We'll be on a better basis next year," he had said. "If my grafting turns out like I think it might, we could be on easy street. Or at least more comfortable," he added with a grin. "Meantime...best to be prepared."

It broke her heart to see him counting his pennies, balancing his checkbook. She had never balanced a checkbook in her life. She wanted to tell him he wouldn't have to, either. That whatever he needed was there, for whatever he wanted to do.

She almost told him. The farm could be his. He could keep on with school.

But something held her back. His enthusiasm in what he was doing. His dream.

His pride.

So she counted the pennies, too. She knew she was spending too much on groceries. Maybe it had to do with never having grocery shopped as well as a tendency for impulse buying. She learned from the Costello women that it was a business venture. That was the day she stopped at Rosalie's and found Sarah sitting with her, the newspaper stretched before them.

"Would you look at this?" Sarah said. "Dishwasher detergent ninety-eight cents. I paid a dollar forty-nine two days ago."

"Honey, I don't buy any staples until I check these ads on Wednesday," Rosalie said.

From that day on, Mel carefully checked Wednesday's ads, and did her grocery shopping on that day. Also she never left Rosalie's without a bag of fresh vegetables from Pedro's garden.

"Your vine-ripened tomatoes are delicious," she said. "And the string beans. I'm going to make Tony plant some vegetables next year. We can't eat flowers."

As she drove home, she thought about that. Next year? Was this skimping going on forever?

Suddenly, she laughed, realizing she didn't care. She was having fun. It was fun visiting with Rosalie and learning how to cook. She even had fun painting the bathroom. Her laughter erupted again as she remembered Tony's thunder-struck face. "You did this! All by yourself!"

"Well, it started with that crumbling plaster," she explained. "Charlie came in when I was over to Rosalie's and I told him about that spot above the tub, you know. And he gave me a bag of stuff and told me how to mix it and he said this kind of paint would be a protective covering after the stuff dried. He gave me a leftover can and a brush and...well, it looked so bright over the tub that...well, I just went berserk and painted the whole wall and the ceiling, too. It didn't take...it's not all that large." She watched that anxious frown, the crease between his eyes, and hastily added, "I wore gloves."

At that he burst out laughing. "I think you needed more covering than gloves," he said, tenderly cleaning her face and arms with kerosene. She could tell he liked it and he sounded proud when he said, "You're quite a woman, Mel Costello," even if he did add, "Next time, honey, let me do it."

But she knew he didn't have time for that kind of thing. And it was like painting the bathroom had given her incentive, power, and a glimmer of what could be done.

She really did go berserk. She took down all those heavy draperies in the living room and let the light in. They didn't need draperies, way out here with no neighbors, and the trees provided enough shade to keep the house cool. This time she bought the paint and brushes, and a roller. No, Pedro brought his own roller when he found out what she was going to do. He really did most of the painting, even if he did grumble as he worked, about the "brother who was fooling around with posies while he did the heavy stuff."

She liked telling Tony that Pedro did it, and didn't at all mind Pedro's warning, "You owe me one."

Then...well, it was like one thing led to another.

"Tony, you remember that first day I came out here with you?" she asked. They were sitting on the back steps and he was massaging her hands with baby oil which he said was more absorbent than Vaseline.

"I remember the day we met. I can still see your hands wrapped around that thermos. So soft and smooth with those oval-shaped, perfectly polished pink nails. Look, you've broken one," he said, rubbing his thumb over the rough edge.

"Oh." She didn't care. She had finally convinced him to let her lend a hand when he set out those new plants. He'd even allowed her to help with his precious rose. They had transplanted it in a big tub which could be set in the garage during a thunderstorm. It might bloom anyday now, Tony said, and he sure didn't want the blossoms crushed.

She liked working with the flowers, and it did give you a good feeling. "You know something,

Tony? I believe it is therapeutic to work with your hands in the earth.''

He grinned. ''Maybe, but it's pretty damaging. And you know something?''

''What?''

''I hate to admit it, but your being a pampered rich girl bugs me. I feel a little paranoid, like…well, like you might just dump me anyday.''

''Never, Tony! Never.'' She reached up and caressed his cheek.

He took her hand, kissed the palm. ''I love your hands. And the way you stand. You look elegant even in those cutoffs and that paint-stained T-shirt. Crazy, huh? I love the pampered rich girl in you, but it scares the hell out of me.''

''Don't worry. I'm not going anywhere. I love the way you pamper me.'' His massaging her hands was more therapeutic than the fifty-dollar manicure she used to get every week. ''Anyway, Tony, I was talking about the day your grandfather fell. Remember?''

''Yeah.''

''It wasn't his arthritis. It was that rug.''

''Huh?''

''I tripped on it myself. Yesterday. And I could see the hardwood floor under it, just like in the rest of the house. Why don't we take up that old carpeting and—''

''We? Damn it! Haven't you heard anything I said? Don't you dare tackle that carpet.''

"I thought maybe you could do it."

"Me! Listen, Mel, there's a hell of a lot more than taking up the carpet. The floor will have to be sanded and—"

"I know. Charlie said he would lend us a sanding machine. It would be just like using a rototiller, wouldn't it?"

He twisted his mouth. "Listen, in a few months, we probably won't even be here."

"Well…" How to explain that? "Any improvement would make the house more valuable, wouldn't it?"

"Anybody who buys this property is not buying the house. It will be demolished. But there will be lots of new houses, and a hell of a lot of concrete," he added with a touch of bitterness. "Let's drop it. I hate to think about it."

She was tempted to tell him then. But she didn't.

She did get the floor sanded, however. She promised Pedro, and Charlie, too, since he had the floor sander, a whole weekend of baby-sitting. Charlie came to help and they finished in one evening. She made a pot of corn chowder just the way Rosalie had taught her, and brought out a bottle of Grandpa Costello's wine to celebrate the beautiful finish.

The old house took on a lift. It seemed more spacious, more beautiful, while retaining the old atmosphere of comfort. A few ferns and flowers from Tony's garden added to the bright cheerfulness. The house seemed to have taken on a charm of its own, or, as Tony put it, "A touch of your elegance."

She had pleased him, and that was satisfaction enough. More even than the wonderful sense of accomplishment. She had done it herself. Mostly...with a little help from the family.

Anyway, she hadn't called in a decorator or a contractor. And she had stayed within the budget.

She was darn proud of herself.

CHAPTER TEN

WHEN the first semblance of a bud appeared on the rosebush, Melody was not at home.

Where the devil was she? He had been watching the bush carefully and had come home because he knew it was beginning to bloom, and he wanted to show her. He wanted to see her eyes light up, hear her exclaim, "Oh, Tony, that's beautiful!" In that special way she had...even if it was just a pot of common peonies. He grinned. Like he was some kind of god, creating what had never been created before.

Okay, okay, he just wanted her here. Wanted her bounding out to meet him, her arms around him, her finger on his crooked tooth. The pure joy of her...her laughter and excitement. Her praise.

And now, here was something worthy of praise, damn it! Something that had never been created before.

Well...not yet, Tony fumed as he studied the tiny kernel that was just the beginning of a bud. No way to tell about the colors he was hoping for.

He'd wait. When it was in full bloom, a bountiful

array of color. More spectacular. He'd show it to her then.

But...damn it! Where the devil was she!

Melody was having lunch with Sarah, Frank's wife.

"This is absolutely delicious," she said as the pizza melted in her mouth. Unlike Virginia-born Rosalie with her Southern cooking, Sarah's cuisine was strictly Italian.

"Glad you like it," Sarah said. She nodded toward the tennis racket. "I see you're prepared for another round with my son."

"I love playing with Don. He's good."

"He ought to be. He lives and breathes tennis. I just shut the door to his room." Sarah sighed. "I keep telling myself that it's a positive and healthy pastime."

"You're right about that," Mel agreed. And it could be more, she thought. The boy had potential. She'd like to take him to the club, where he might get some pointers from the tennis pro. Just like she wanted to take Pedro's kids sailing on Jake's boat.

But...not yet. She wasn't quite sure what restrained her. Didn't know why she felt it wasn't quite time to mix her two worlds. Later... But, not yet.

"At least he's got a part-time job this summer. City Rec," Sarah said. She glanced at the clock. "He'll be here in a minute."

"Good," Mel said. "After this lunch I need the exercise." It was fun playing with Don. And he claimed he was getting a few pointers from her, that his serve and backhand had really been improved.

By the time he heard the old Ford coming down the lane, it was late in the day. He had just closed the doors of the barn to protect the rosebush and the other delicate potted plants he kept there. Thunderclouds were forming and it looked like a big storm. He hurried to meet her.

She got out of the car, looking like a fashion model in that short white dress that hardly covered her bottom. Tennis, he thought, realizing he was glad she had been having some fun. But more glad to see her home, to see the wind whipping her hair around her pixie face just as it had on that very first day. She was adorable.

Before he could take her in his arms, she was at the passenger side of the car.

He couldn't believe it. She was releasing a squirming toddler from the car seat.

"What the dickens are you doing with her?"

"The floor sanding, remember? I promised to baby-sit. Charlie and Leona are going to a dance at his lodge, and I said I'd keep her overnight. Here, you take her."

He swung the girl up in his arms. "Well, don't stare at me like that. I'm not happy, either. I want a visit from you like I want a hole in the head," he said, tickling her while he talked. But even as the baby giggled and squirmed with delight, he still grumbled. "Where the devil are you going to sleep? I'm damned if I'm going up to the attic for that old crib."

"You won't have to," Mel said. "Give her to me while you take the playpen out of the trunk. Leona says she climbs out of it when she's awake, but it ought to make a safe enough bed."

As they walked toward the house loaded with the toddler and her paraphernalia, he said, "So that's where you were all day? At Charlie's?"

"No. I was there just to pick her up on my way home. I had lunch with Sarah, and then I played tennis with Don. Tony, do you know how good that boy is?" She rattled on, telling him about her day, all the while keeping busy feeding and fondling the little girl.

By the time they got the overactive child settled in her improvised bed beside theirs, they were too exhausted to do anything but crawl into bed themselves.

So much for the news about my not-yet-blooming rose, he thought, as he held his wife close and listened to the storm raging outside. Just as well I waited. This is her night.

But it hadn't been so bad, he admitted. She was a good baby, and knew them pretty well. She only cried once, late in the night. Mel slipped on a robe and rocked her in Grandma's old rocking chair. She looked like a Madonna, Tony thought, as flashes of lightning played against her face, nuzzled so lovingly against the baby's head.

Someday, he thought, she will hold our child like that. And was surprised how touched he was by the thought.

A week later the roses bloomed. Three long, sturdy stems held one bud each. Oval-shaped resplendent buds with high centers and the multitude of petals that would soon open to display the myriad of colors just as he had dreamed them. He had done it! Tears burned his eyes, there was a lump in his throat, and he was glad neither of his brothers was there to see him.

Later in the evening, he called Mel down to see his "surprise." One rose in a tall bud vase stood in the center of the table surrounded by candles. Its kaleidoscope of colors, peach, salmon and lavender with little swirls of yellow, danced in their light.

Melody stood transfixed, her eyes wide with awe. "Tony. Oh, Tony..." she breathed. She stared in deep appreciation. "It's so absolutely beautiful. So many colors. How did you do it?"

"Like it's always been done since 1867."

"Huh?"

"That's true," he said. "Before then all the roses grown here and in Europe were pink, white, or red. When these were crossed with the yellow tea rose of China, the first hybrid tea rose, called LaFrance, was developed in 1867. Since then...well, you know. We have our modern hybrids in several colors, or mixed colors. Just a matter of grafting, crossing, and...'' He stopped, embarrassed by the admiration in her eyes. Was that why he was always parading his knowledge before her? Just to see that look?

''And that's what you've been doing! You're so clever, Tony. This one's so different. I've never seen any like it.''

He smiled. ''Thank you. That's the point.''

''And you did it. You really did. All that grafting and pruning to create this...this... Oh, Tony it's so beautiful. I love it.''

''I'm glad you like my Melody rose.''

Her eyes shot to him. ''Melody? For me?''

''From one beauty to another,'' he said, handing her a glass of champagne.

''Flatterer!'' she said, touching her glass to his.

''It's not flattery, sweet. You are as beautiful. But that's not why I gave it your name.''

''No?''

''No. I named it Melody because it is you.''

''What!''

He pointed to the rose. ''See that melody of colors?''

She nodded, her eyes twinkling as she took a sip of champagne.

''A melody of the many yous.''

She gave a gurgle of laughter. ''Go on, Tony. I'm just me.''

"No. You're more. You're a mother to my grandmother, you're a fighter with my dad, sparring with him like nobody else in the family dares to. You're a playmate for Pedro's kids, and a tennis partner for Don. You've got a stamp of elegance you can't lose, even when you're wielding a paint-brush. And hell, you're a million things to me." He set her glass on the table beside his. He took her in his arms and whispered against her ear. "You're a supportive, caring, loving, shamelessly passionate woman who has made me the happiest man on earth."

"Tony, oh, Tony," she said against his lips. "That's the nicest thing you've ever said... No. It is absolutely the most wonderful, sweetest, most marvelous compliment I've ever received. I love you."

"And I love you," he said, wondering if he could ever make her know how much she meant to him. She made him feel like...well, like he was somebody, and what he was doing was okay. Great even. His brothers called him a posy pusher, and nobody in his family was altogether pleased with what he did. Nobody really knew how much he liked what he was doing, how much he loved his flowers.

Mel knew. Mel loved him. She was the best thing that had ever happened to him.

The horticultural conference was held at a resort in Atlantic City. They traveled there in style, with the

Melody rosebush on the floor in the back of Grandpa Costello's old Ford. They went a day earlier to get it set up in the big showroom among a huge variety of plants, and to be in place for the judging. The prizes were to be announced at the banquet on the last night. Melody was nervous. She was sure Tony's tea rose was the most beautiful, most unusual tea rose in the place. But would the judges know it?

She was surprised that Tony seemed not at all nervous. In fact, he appeared more relaxed than she'd ever seen him.

But, of course. Why not? He wasn't working, and he wasn't thinking about what had to be done the next day…or the next minute. She liked seeing him so much at ease, without that distracted look he often had when they were at family gatherings.

It occurred to her that this was the first time she had seen him in a social situation among others than family. But he was sure at home here. He knew many people attending the conference, and proudly introduced his wife. They joined others for lunch, dinner and impromptu conversational groups. Mostly plant talk. Mulching, soil preservation, and crossbreeding in scientific terms that transcended her meager knowledge. But Tony was right with them.

Of course! This was his field. These were his colleagues. He might work like a dirt farmer, but he was a professional. She listened as he held his own with learned professors and scientists, agreeing, disputing, or simply exchanging knowledge. She could tell they respected his opinion.

"You must be getting pretty tired of all this horticultural business," he said one afternoon after a particularly heated discussion.

"Not at all," she protested. And she wasn't. She was almost bursting with pride.

"No? Well, chalk up another you," he said, grinning. "Patience." He kissed her right there in the crowded hotel lobby. "You ought to have some fun though. Dr. Lindstrom asked if we would join him and his wife for a round of golf in the morning. Do you want to? Or do you play?" he asked, as an after thought.

Of course she played golf. But did he?

He must have caught the amazement and question in her expression, for he chuckled. "Honey, I caddied my way through college. Couldn't help but play."

He played well, too. Better than anyone else in the foursome, though he said he hadn't touched a club in over a year. And it was his exuberance that made the game so much fun. Tony was good-humored by nature, always teasing and joking even at work. But it was good to see him so vibrant and enthusiastic, as totally involved in play as he usually was in work. Good to see him just having fun. They also found a little time to surf in the ocean and sun on the beach. It was like a honeymoon, which, come to think of it, they'd never had.

But that last night at the banquet. Her husband receiving the award and all those approbations for his development of the Melody rose.

Oh, she had known it was beautiful and different, and had been thrilled that he named it after her. But she had had no idea that it was such a spectacular achievement.

All this official recognition! Scientific commendation. Her eyes filled with happy tears as she listened to words of praise from notables in the field.

This was her husband, thanking them for the acknowledgment, answering their questions with unassuming candor. So modest. So handsome in that dark suit and the shirt and tie she had selected.

This was the first time she had seen him in a coat and tie. Except for one hot moment, she thought, at their disastrous wedding! Something between a sob and a giggle caught in her throat as she thought of that day. Only a few short months, but it seemed a lifetime ago.

Now Tony was taking her hand, pulling her into the admiring group that surrounded him. One or two of the men pressed their cards into his hand, asked for his. When and where could he be contacted? They'd like an appointment as soon as possible. Had he made any commitments? On and on...

"What was that all about?" she asked when they were alone.

"Floral marketing companies," he answered. "They'd like exclusive rights to the patent."

"Patent?"

"For my Melody rose."

"Oh." A rose patent. "Tony," she exclaimed. "You'd better get one right away. Where did you say you send it? Who do you see?"

He laughed. "Don't worry, hon. It's all been taken care of. I turned it over sometime ago to this law firm recommended by my botany professor. Gaston and Ferber. They deal almost exclusively with plant patents."

So. She learned something else about her husband. He was also a man of business.

CHAPTER ELEVEN

IT WAS, she decided, time they gave a party. A real party. All the members of Tony's family had been over from time to time. But not altogether. And none of her family. Except her father, that one time.

This would be a big party. Not only their families, but other people. Charlie and his wife. Link and other florists that dealt with Tony. And some of Tony's professors. It would be a celebration for Tony. He had done a big thing, and she wanted everybody to know about it.

The house was in as good order as she could make it. And it was still summer. They could spread outdoors. That is, if it didn't rain, she thought, crossing her fingers.

She would call that caterer Dad always uses...

No, she wouldn't. She and Sarah and Rosalie could do the food. Marie would help with the serving. And Frank's boys would serve the drinks.

Plans flew 'round and 'round in her mind. Got bigger when Tony told her the good news. A marketing firm had made an offer.

"A big offer," he said.

"Tony, that's wonderful!" She looked up from

her seat at the kitchen table where she was making notes for the party. "Are you going to take it?"

"Well, Gaston said we ought to wait. He's sure there will be some counteroffers."

"Really!" She made a note on her pad as another idea popped into her head. She'd invite some representatives from marketing firms. Display Tony's rose. Mix business with pleasure.

"Gaston's already contacting others. He says an auction would really boost the price."

What firms marketed flowers? She'd ask her Dad. Flowers were not his field, but marketing was. He was in the know about who marketed anything.

"What do you think, hon?"

"What?" She'd been thinking so hard, she hadn't heard him.

"You think we should take this offer or wait?"

"Wait, of course. What's the hurry? If there's a chance for a better offer...?"

"But this is enough for a down payment on this place, if I can swing it. The Taylor firm has an option, but there's no sign of rezoning yet, and they might be a little tired of waiting. Ten thousand a month is an awful lot of money for something that might not happen. Maybe, if we made an offer now, before—"

"Oh, Tony, you don't have to worry about that." She smiled. Now was the time to tell him.

"What do you mean?"

"I mean, the farm is already yours." She told

him, anticipating the relief, excitement, pleasure. Now he could really settle in. Build the greenhouses or whatever.

He stared at her. He looked anything but pleased. He looked...displeased? Mad?

"What?" he said. "You...you hold the option on the farm?"

She nodded, swallowing the lump in her throat. Surely now it was all right. Now that he...

"You've been shelling out ten thousand dollars a month on this place for the past three months?"

Again she nodded. Apprehensive.

"You lied to me."

She shook her head.

"You told me you were not going to touch your father's money."

"I didn't. It was mine."

"Yours! You told me you didn't have much."

"I didn't...don't." Not as much as her father had. "Just the trust fund my grandmother left me."

"How much?"

"Thirty million."

"Thirty million dollars?" he repeated in a slow, unbelieving whisper.

"I didn't touch it. Not the capital. Just a little of the interest."

It was as if he hadn't heard her. "Your father knew this. That was why his snotty put-down! The smirk on his face when I was spouting off about how I was going to support myself and you!"

"You did support us. We've been living off what you've earned, haven't we?"

"Not by a long shot, baby. Not when you put a ten-thousand-dollar-a-month roof over our head."

"You didn't get a dime of that money. It all went to your grandparents." She threw her pencil to the table and stood up to face him. "And I don't see why you're so mad. They need the money, you need the farm."

"I'm mad because you lied to me."

"Because you're so damn hopped up about doing your own thing on your own money. Macho. Senseless. You wouldn't have stayed with me one minute if you knew you had to use one penny that was mine."

"That's not true. If you'd been straight with me. If you'd told me—"

"Ha! You'd have gone up in smoke like you're doing right now over…over…" She hesitated. How could she put it? "Tony, my dad says any good businessman uses other people's money. This was just a small capital investment which is sorely needed. It's a pittance. Nothing!"

"Nothing?" The fire in his eyes told her she had cut him to the quick. "Why, of course. I forgot. You're Miss Rich Bitch! Well, thanks. But no thanks. You can keep your pittance and all that goes with it."

"Tony, I didn't mean… Oh, you're so bull-headed! So hopped up about—"

"Right. I am hopped up about my own money. And ever will be. And I don't like being lied to. This marriage has been a sham from the very first day. I wonder what else is in the woodwork that I don't know about."

"Tony…" She reached out to touch him.

He jerked away, turned from her and slammed out of the room.

Mel started to follow. Stopped short.

What exactly had she said to make him so burned up?

All right. Perhaps the wrong choice of words. "Pittance. Nothing."

She meant only to emphasize that it was no big deal. Which it wasn't, for Pete's sake!

He's so sensitive.

Well, damn it, I'm sensitive, too.

Oh, hell! I'm sick of this guilt trip about being rich. I'm sick of tiptoeing around it…counting pennies and scrubbing floors just to salvage his stupid pride.

Tony's right. This is a sham marriage, and I'm tired of playing a game. If he can't accept me as I am, then the hell with it!

She stormed out of the kitchen. She marched right past Tony who was staring moodily out of the living room window, and mounted the stairs. In the bedroom, she pulled out her overnight case, and feverishly began to throw things in.

Stopped. What was the point? She had left ten

times more of her things at home than she'd ever brought here. Must have known this was only temporary, she thought as she closed the half-filled bag and marched back downstairs.

The bag caught his attention. "Where are you going?"

"Out of your life, thank you very much. I'm ending this facade."

"Melody—"

"I'm taking the car, but don't worry. I'll send it right back."

"You don't have to."

She turned to face him. "I don't need anything of yours, Tony Costello. As you say, I'm a rich bitch, and I can damn well take care of myself." She ran down the steps, got into the car to send it speeding down the lane.

Tony stood on the top step. Mixed emotions. Mad. Confused.

Concerned. Damn it, damn it, she was too mad to be driving!

But he had been too late to stop her. It would be more dangerous to chase after her. Anyway, this sham has to end.

She mopped at the blinding tears with her fists as she drove down the highway. Before she got home, she stopped and took a Handi Wipes from her purse. When she reached her house, her face was clean and bright. Her eyes were very bright, also, and very wide open as if she didn't dare blink.

She stopped in front of the garage where Leo, her father's chauffeur, was polishing the cars.

He nodded as if her appearance, wearing a pair of frayed cutoffs and driving an old Ford was a common occurrence. "Miss Sands. Oh, no, you're Mrs.—"

"You got it right. Sands. How are you, Leo?"

"Fine, just fine. And you?"

"Okay. Look, would you please take this car back for me?" He nodded, and she gave him the keys and directions. "Get Pete or somebody to follow and drive you back," she said as she went into the house.

The house was very quiet. Where was everybody?

Her father was in the den. "Why, hello!" He lowered his newspaper to look up at her, switched to the overnight case she still carried...like a badge. "You're...er...home?"

"For good. And don't you dare say I told you so."

"Oh, I...well... For good, eh?"

"I'm never going back there. He's impossible!" She threw down her bag and began to pace the floor, muttering to herself. She was glad she hadn't mentioned the party to anybody, not even Rosalie. Hadn't started preparations, invited anyone. Nothing hanging over, incomplete. A clean break.

Her life with Tony Costello was over with. Finished. Kaput!

She heard her father clear his throat. "What about it?"

"What about what?"

"I suggested dinner at the club. It's about that time, and since Cook's away…"

That's right. There had been no sign of her. "Where is Cook?"

"Haven't you heard a word I've said. I told you. She's gone to visit her sister in Alameda."

"Oh."

"So what about it? Do you want to go to the club or maybe to the Classic?"

The thought of the Classic made her heart turn over. Tony's ferns. The wedding lunch they hadn't had. "I don't feel like dressing," she said. Why were they talking about dinner, anyway? She wasn't hungry. "Well, I could send Leo out to fetch something."

"Leo's not here, and I'm not…" She stopped. If she said she wasn't hungry, he might go out by himself, and she didn't want to be alone. "I'll fix something."

"You?"

His incredulity made her madder than she already was. "Yes, me!"

He actually laughed. "Honey, I'm not in the mood for bacon and eggs."

"Steak? Lamb chops? What do you want?"

"Oh, well…anything you can whip up."

"I can whip up anything you like. What do you think I've been doing for the last three months? I'll see what's here." She stalked into the kitchen and began slamming things around. She sure wasn't going to hide away upstairs and do something stupid, like cry.

Thirty minutes later, they were both seated at the kitchen table, and her father was eating with gusto. "This is absolutely delicious," he said.

"Thanks." She knew that. Mashed potatoes fluffy enough to melt in your mouth. The chops were succulent, browned to a turn. Lamb chops. Tony's favorite. She had often stretched the budget to include them. She stretched her eyes wide, holding back the tears.

"You know something, Mel? I think you're a better cook than Cook."

"Yes." Almost anybody was better than Cook. And she had liked cooking…for Tony. It had been fun. She poked at her salad, not daring to brush away the tears that were now streaming down her face.

Samuel Sands couldn't pretend not to see them. He put down his fork. "Mel, I'm sorry."

"It's all right. I'll get over it." She mopped at the tears, as if relieved not to have to pretend anymore. "I'm not going to let three months with Tony Costello mess up my whole life."

"Of course not."

"Only, it was…so good between us, Dad. It really was. I thought he was happy. I was. It was fun. I didn't even mind all the scrubbing and cleaning, and watching every penny. And I really liked cooking. I like his family, too. Even if all the men are a bunch of chauvinistic pigs." She gave a choking laugh. "Well, they all come on that way. But when you get to know them, they're…well, like Rosalie says, as soft as cotton. Loving, and well, just protective."

"I'll buy that," Sands agreed. "Your Tony tried to protect you from me. I can see him now, standing in that kitchen, warning me not to badger his wife."

"He did…didn't he?" She tried to smile through her tears, and he could see the warmth, the tenderness in her eyes. Then she looked troubled. "He said the way you looked at him that day was…well, like a put-down. And now, I can see why he feels so embarrassed. I…well, I did lie to him."

"Oh?"

"He was so mad when those reporters nabbed us after our wedding, and he found out I have money. He was going to leave me and I didn't want him to. I told him I wasn't going to touch a penny of your money, that I wanted to prove something to you and to myself."

"And what about your own money?"

"I…well, I kinda glossed over that. I told him it wasn't much. We could save it for a rainy day."

"I see." His lips twitched. "And I take it he suddenly found out how much?"

"Today. You see, and this was before we married, before I ever knew he would ask me to, I got Jake's wife to take an option on that farm."

"I know all about that."

"You do?"

"I knew and I knew that Tony didn't know."

"Of course. When you left us that morning I was sure that wasn't the end. You were going to have Tony investigated from top to bottom."

"You didn't think I'd let you get stuck with a man who was just after your money, did you? Remember Dirk?"

"Oh, Dirk," she said, like he was a fly on the wall. "And you found out all about Tony, didn't you?"

"I did."

"How honest he is, and how hard he works. You can't imagine. He's always working, days at those odd jobs he takes. Early in the morning and late at night with his flowers. He loves working with flowers. I do, too, when he lets me. He's got this thing about my hands. He's always massaging them." She frowned. "Stupid. I could get a manicure every day if I wanted to. But he's so touchy about my money. I thought he wouldn't be after his great success."

"Success?"

"Oh, yes. Tony has developed this rose. He

named it the Melody rose." She paused, a tender faraway expression on her face. "It is the most beautiful flower I've ever seen. And everybody is so excited about it. At the conference people were giving him their cards, and one firm has already offered to buy his patent. Tony had already been negotiating for a patent. He's a good businessman, too."

"Not a very good one if he takes that offer."

She stared at him. "You know about that, too?"

"Of course. And I've already been in touch with Gaston, his lawyer. I've got a big hunk of stock with Tampa Florists, and we're offering a bigger bonus, plus a share of the royalties."

"Oh, no, Dad! Don't!" She looked positively horrified.

"Why not? This is business. That thing has potential."

"It might seem that... If Tony knew you had anything to do with it... If it looked anything like a handout, he'd never take me back! Never!"

"That doesn't matter, does it? Since you're never going back anyway."

She straightened, eyes flashing. "Right. I'm never going back into that...that sham! Sneaking, lying, pretending. Like having money is a sin."

CHAPTER TWELVE

TONY sat on the steps. For the first time in his life, he didn't feel like doing anything.

She's gone.

Well, you always knew she'd leave you, didn't you?

Yeah. Too special for him. He'd felt it in his bones. Even on that very first day when he didn't know who or what she was. Standing there holding that thermos with the wind whipping her hair. He had wanted to grab her and run. He couldn't believe it when she said she'd go out for a burger.

Even after she had married him, it didn't seem for real. That night...standing like a ghost at the door of his old room... "I love you, Tony. Doesn't that count?" He'd only half believed it, even then. He'd grabbed her and held on, like she might disappear.

Well, she's disappeared now, buddy!

Good. Face it. We're not right for each other. Out of balance. I'm cramping her style, and damn it, she's cramping mine!

Makes me look like a fourteen-carat fool! There I am crowing over a measly twenty-five thousand dollar offer! "Think about it, honey. It could be a down payment on this place…if we can swing it, if we can get around that option that some big muckety-muck has laid on it.''

And then she hits me with the hot brick. She's the muckety-muck. ''It's already yours, Tony. I bought it a long time ago,'' she says. Handing me the farm like a present all done up in pretty paper. Nothing. A pittance.

Jeez!

She didn't mean it for a put-down.

I know. I'm sorry I said what I said to her. Sorry I acted like I did. But when you feel like a fool, you act like one.

We're bad for each other. Mismatched. It's good she's gone.

Gone. I won't think about it.

I better prune those roses.

Water the plants in the barn.

No. Better drop in on Gaston. He says he's got a better deal.

He was still sitting on the steps when he heard the car coming up the lane.

His spirit lifted as his ears perked. The old Ford. Maybe… Was she returning?

But she wasn't driving the Ford. And there was another car following. A sleek silver sports car…an expensive one.

Like a slap in the face!

''Thank you,'' he said to the man who handed

him the keys. He watched him get in the passenger seat of the Jaguar. Watched the smooth departure.

Then he got up and went to tend the roses.

"Okay, Tony. Give! What's going on?" Pedro stood before him like some damn avenging judge, itching to pronounce sentence.

Rosalie was right beside him. "Yeah, Tony. Where's Mel? She hasn't been around, and every time I call—"

"We've split."

"What do you mean...split?"

"Split! Separated. Quit." Damn it, he had avoided this confrontation as long as he could. "Can't you understand plain English. It's over. She's gone."

"Oh, Tony, what did you do?"

"What did *I* do? Rosalie, this whole thing has been a farce, right from the beginning. You know that."

"I don't know anything of the kind. You seemed so happy. After that first day..."

"That first day. Yeah! You were there. You know what happened."

"But that was three months ago. I know you were hurt. But I thought you had gotten over it."

Over the hurt, maybe. But not the character-shattering embarrassment. "You don't ever get over something like that, Rosie. You heard the questions… 'How does it feel to be married to an heiress?' "

"Yes, but…"

"I didn't marry an heiress. As far as I knew. And did you hear what that woman asked her? 'Why do these types of men appeal to you?' Damn it to hell, I'm not a type. And I'm not a sex object to be bought or sold by any woman!"

"Oh, Tony, why in heaven's name are you going back to that? You and Mel…"

"Wait, Rosie." Pedro touched his wife, shook his head. "Look, isn't there something left? Why don't you fix Tony a plate? He must be hungry."

"No. Don't bother," Tony protested. It was late. She had washed dishes and put the children in bed. But he allowed his brother to lead him back to the kitchen. He sat at the table, breathing in the smell of food she was warming…honey-baked ham, collard greens. He was hungry. When had he last eaten? He tried to remember. But all he could remember was that Mel had been gone for three days, and—

"Here you are, brother, dear," Rosalie said, placing a steaming plate before him.

"Thank you." Just the smell of it warmed him. "You know something, Rosalie? You're a damn good cook."

"Mel's a good cook, too. She—"

"Tony, you ought to see that Patsy swim!"

Pedro broke in, with a significant glance at his wife. "She cuts through that water like a fish."

Rosalie, taking the cue, followed his lead. Tony enjoyed the first real meal he'd had in three days, and listened to their chatter about the antics of the children. He realized he was hungry for something else. Companionship. Family.

And...he hated going back to that empty farm. He'd never felt so alone in his life.

It was after Rosalie had taken away his empty plate, and they sat with mugs of hot coffee that Pedro invited him to open up. "Okay, Tony. Shoot. What went wrong?"

"Everything. To begin with, I found I've been living off her for the past three months."

"That's not true," Rosalie said. "I know that for a fact. I've seen her checking the grocery ads, counting every penny, trying to make sure there'd be enough left for whatever you'd need for the farm."

"Yeah. The farm. How about that?"

"Huh?"

He told them.

They were both silent for a moment, trying to take it in. Then Rosalie spoke. "I can understand that. You know how worried Grandma was about Grandpa and those stairs, and she wasn't able to take care of him. Mel must have seen they needed the money, and since she had it... Look, it was like that time Frank broke his leg, and you and Pedro pitched in and picked up the slack till he was back on his feet.''

"It's not like that at all. Frank had an emergency and we did something about it, all open and above-board. Mel said not one word to me about this. If she'd been open, if she'd told me straight out—''

"Ha! You'd have gone up in smoke just like you're doing now and you know it!''

He stared at her. Just what Mel had said...almost the exact words. His mouth twisted. "Well, that's not all she lied about.''

"Oh?'' Pedro, whose eyes had been focused on the table as if in deep study, looked up.

"She gave me this spiel about how she wasn't going to use any of her father's money. I didn't ask her, mind you. It was her own idea. We would live off what I earned and save the little she had for a rainy day.''

"So? You did, didn't you?'' Rosalie asked. "What's the big lie?''

"The *little* she has. Like thirty million dollars.''

Rosalie choked.

Pedro whistled. "Thirty million dollars?''

"Some trust fund her grandmother left her. She handled the option out of a small portion of the interest. How does that grab you?''

Pedro looked like he was still trying to grab hold of the facts. "She told you she had this trust fund. And you never thought—''

"She never mentioned the word trust. And no, I

didn't think. A little? Maybe a few thousands. My mind doesn't run to millions. Not even one, much less thirty!''

Pedro nodded. ''I see what you mean.''

''Yeah. How'd you like to live under that shadow? I'd be dancing to her tune for the rest of my life.''

''Pretty nice shadow.'' They both turned to Rosalie, who was grinning from ear to ear. ''Imagine! Thirty million dollars. I wouldn't mind dancing a jig to that!'' She got up, twirled around to prove it.

''Stop it, Rosalie, before you bump into something and hurt yourself. Sit down, and let's talk this over.''

She came back to her chair. ''Yeah, let's talk about it. I'd like to know who's dancing to whose tune!''

Tony stared at her. ''What do you mean?''

''I mean if I had thirty million dollars, I sure wouldn't be acting like a scrubwoman. Not even for Pedro whom I love as much as Mel loves you.''

''Are you saying—?''

''That's exactly what I'm saying. I've never seen a woman work so hard to be poor.''

''Look I never asked—''

''Oh, no, you never asked. You just marched off in a huff, all hurt and embarrassed about her having all that money, and how dare she lie about it! Spouting off about an annulment and leaving her alone on her wedding night. Right after you had promised to love and keep her for *richer or poorer* the rest of your life, you walked out and left her all alone, bawling her eyes out!''

"Look, it wasn't like that. We had words, and—''

"Oh, yes, you did. Cause I got her on the phone right after you left her. She was so hurt and so scared because you were mad and were never coming back to her, so choked up she could hardly talk. I told her you'd come 'round. I told her to just cuddle up and love you and... You know something, Tony Costello! I wish I'd told her to kick you in your pants. All this much ado about money and skipping love altogether!''

"Well, I...'' Tony, who had been transfixed by Rosalie, suddenly turned to Pedro who was laughing his head off. "What's so funny?''

"Nothing.'' Pedro tried to stifle the laughter. "Well, just the situation. Now, wait.'' He pushed Tony, who had started to stand, back into his chair. "Believe me, I know how you feel. I'm a Costello, too. But Rosalie has a point. She's right about Mel. She's been busting her butt, trying to please you. I know. I've seen her in action. She'll not be asking you to dance to her tune. She's not that type. And...'' His eyes began to twinkle and he almost broke into laughter again. "Well, face it, buddy. Thirty million dollars ain't exactly poison. I think you could learn to live with it.''

* * *

He didn't want to go home. Which was one of the reasons he had stopped here, he thought as he pulled out of Pedro's driveway. He couldn't stay at a motel like he had done for the past two nights. Well, he had had to be in the city early for work, hadn't he? He glanced at his watch. Not all that late. He could stop for a drink. But hanging around in bars wasn't his thing.

Anyway, face it, buddy! You gotta go home sometime.

And things needed doing. Like watering before everything dried up.

But there's nobody there. Not even Cocoa. He had left the dog at the vet.

Mel's not there.

Damn! Damn! Damn! How could he miss her so much? It was a deep-seated ache that wouldn't go away. That took the joy out of everything.

Crazy. It hadn't been like that before. He'd been contented. Busy. Odd jobs in the city during the day, school at night. And he'd had fun, dated a few times. That girl in his botany class at school…what was her name? He couldn't remember and didn't care.

And yeah, he'd been busy here, he thought as he pulled into the farm. He had already started his nursery. He had set out some shrubs and perennials, potted the lilies for the Easter market.

Lilies. He remembered the blooming plants in a multitude of pots set out on his improvised tables in the barn. Saw Mel beside him, her gorgeous hair in disarray, a smudge of dirt on her nose. Watering, wrapping, lifting the pots into the truck.

You're right, Pedro. I've seen her in action, too.

They weren't even married then. That was the first day he had brought her to the farm. The first time he had kissed her, right there in the barn.

He parked the truck, mounted the steps and went into the house. He stood for a moment, over-whelmed by the emptiness.

Then he moved quickly, to switch on lamps. As if the lights would radiate some of the brightness that was Mel.

And yes, she was reflected in the bright painted wall, the polished floor, the afghan on the sofa that still held the faint aroma of the perfume she always used.

But she wasn't there, and the emptiness mocked him.

She wasn't in the bedroom, either, though her presence filled the room. A robe thrown across the bed, a slipper askew on the floor, a bracelet on the dresser. The scent of her perfume was stronger here.

But not as strong as the scent of roses. Old roses with that magic old rose fragrance that had en-twined with the magic of their love on that first night. And every night since.

These roses, she had put there three days ago. They were long past their full bloom now, their dying petals scattered on the polished surface of the dresser. But it was as if in death, their fragrance grew richer, a strong, potent reminder of a love that refused to die.

He could not stop loving Mel. He stood in the room that was theirs, breathing in the fragrance. Remembering...

Her laughter... Musical and delightful as she searched among the sheets... "Where are the petals you should have put here to entice me?" The irrepressible chuckles mocking herself whenever she was puzzled or didn't do something right. He missed her laughter.

He missed her. Her bolstering "you're so wonderful" trust that gave him such confidence, made him feel like he could conquer the world. Her vivacious buoyant spirit, her zest for life, that made each day a bright adventure. He missed the warm, passionate woman in his arms who made each night a bit of heaven.

How had he let her walk out of his life!

Money.

Something she had. Not what she was.

He sat on the bed, feeling a little stunned. Not once, during the three months they lived together, had he thought of her money. Not since that first day when those news people had rammed it down his throat. Afterward... Well...he just hadn't thought about money. He had been totally involved in the warm, loving, lovable woman who nestled into his heart and became an irrevocable part of his life.

How could he live without her?

He picked up the phone.

It kept ringing and ringing.

She burrowed deep into her pillow, trying to shut out the sound. She was asleep at last. From pure exhaustion.

The ringing... Why didn't somebody shut it off!

It continued. Penetrating. Demanding. Arousing.

She blinked at the clock on the bedside table— 2:00 a.m.

It was her line, her phone that was ringing. She picked it up.

"Mel?"

Tony. Her heart turned over. Her fingers tightened on the phone. She had hoped, waited for his call. And now...

"Mel? Mel, are you there?" He sounded demanding.

He had found out.

It would start all over again. The anger. The accusations.

She couldn't bear it. Not now.

She replaced the phone.

CHAPTER THIRTEEN

SHE was fully awake now. She got out of bed and pulled on her robe.

She knew he would be angry. He didn't have to wake her up in the middle of the night to tell her so!

This was the first night she had been able to get to sleep at all. It was as if Grandma Costello's words today had soothed her, made her feel she had done something right.

And she had, hadn't she? What else could she do? After Judy's call. She couldn't leave his grandparents hanging, and she wanted to be sure they had enough to be comfortable for the rest of their lives.

Okay, okay, she had wanted something else, too. She wanted to make sure Tony had the farm, whatever happened between them. She knew he wouldn't like it. The option was bad enough. But the farm, signed, sealed, and delivered *to him* was like a red flag, goading a bull that had already been stabbed.

That was why the call. For a moment, when she heard him calling her name, she had thought...

She jerked the cord on her robe tight. Angry. Just the sound of his voice could send her senses reeling.

She had waited for that call, waited by the phone, never leaving the house for two whole days. Hoping he had calmed down, and they could talk reasonably, make some decisions.

No. That wasn't right. She hadn't wanted him calm at all. She wanted him wild with despair and loneliness, as hungry for her as she was for him. She wanted to hear him begging her to come back. Telling her nothing mattered but their love, that he couldn't live without her. Something like that, she thought as she made her way downstairs.

Maybe a cup of hot chocolate...

No. No way could she get back to sleep.

In the kitchen, she reached for the percolator. Coffee. Strong. She had to think.

How had Tony found out so soon? It was just today, this afternoon...

Papers had to be processed and...

Did they need his signature?

No. Preston had said all she had to do was deed it over to him and that was that.

She had phoned Preston, her lawyer, right after Judy called.

"Mel, I've been trying to reach you," Judy had said. "I called the farm and got no answer."

"I've been out a lot. Glad you caught me here," she said, not wanting to tell Judy, or anyone, that she had moved out. Left Tony. That would make it sound so...so final.

"I got a call from Jim," Judy said. "Mrs.

Costello phoned him. Another firm has made an offer on the farm. Jim wants to know if you want to exercise the option or bow out.''

Of course she had to exercise the option. So she had immediately gone to Preston and had him draw up a bill of sale, the price to be filled in. She would outbid the other firm, no matter how much. She also had him draw up papers, deeding the farm to Tony. She had taken the papers out to the retirement home herself.

To her surprise, Grandma Costello was not surprised.

''I thought all along that you held that option,'' she said, when she was alone with Mel. Business over, Mel had taken the older woman out to pick up some toiletries and they had stopped for a late lunch at a nearby tearoom.

''Why did you think so?'' Mel asked.

''I knew you. It's your nature to be helpful. You were always helping Tony with his flowers. And you came out to help us pack and make the move. That was a big move for us. Having you and Meg there made it so much easier to get settled in a new place. Did I ever thank you?''

''Of course you did. Many times. But you didn't need to. I always enjoy being with you.'' Still... ''That was no reason to connect me with the option,'' she said. She had gone to a deal of trouble to conceal the facts.

''Oh, I didn't. Not at first. But afterward...when

there was all that fuss in the news and it came out about your money. Well, I just put two and two together. I knew that was just the kind of thing you would do.''

Mel shook her head, marveling at her perception. No one else had suspected, not even Tony. ''And you never said anything.''

''I didn't dare. Well, I—'' She broke off, frowning. ''To tell the truth, I was really upset. All that hullabaloo after your wedding, and Tony just finding out. I was sure he would blow his top. Men are so funny about…well, you know.''

''Yes.'' She certainly knew that.

''I held my breath, so afraid it would cause a breakup between the two of you. I sure didn't want that to happen. You are so right for each other. I could tell that first day when you came out to the farm with him. That was the day Al fell and scared the living daylights out of me. Remember?''

Mel nodded, remembering every detail. The old man lying across the steps, cursing. The dog jumping all over him. The woman standing by, helpless and anxious. Remembered her words later in the barn… ''I've got to sell, Tony. I'm so worried about Al.''

The memory seemed a kind of benediction. I'm glad I did it. Glad I made it easy for them to be comfortable and for Tony to have the farm.

''You were so sweet, Mel. You pitched right in,'' Mrs. Costello said, as if confirming Mel's thoughts.

"You helped with Al, and helped Tony with his lilies. Like you were already one of the family."

Yes. That was the way she had felt, that first day, the minute Tony drove into the farm. Happy, peaceful, as if she had come home.

"Yes, I liked you from the first, Mel. When I heard about your wedding...on TV mind you, which I didn't like! Still, I was glad you were married, but scared, too. I know these men. Been living with one for fifty-six years. I was sure Tony was going to act a fool about the money." She shook her head, took a deep breath. "He didn't, thank goodness. I'm so relieved that you are still as lovey-dovey as ever."

She doesn't know. Tony hasn't told her. Mel opened her eyes wide, holding back the tears. How could my life be so messed up and she doesn't know!

"You must be excited about this new rose Tony has developed," Mrs. Costello said as she complacently sipped her tea. "Isn't he wonderful with those flowers!"

"Yes, he is."

"I'm glad he enjoys it. Work is such a pleasure when you like what you're doing."

"Yes."

"You know something, Mel?" The older woman reached over to touch her hand. "I'm glad about your money, too."

"You are?"

Mrs. Costello laughed. "Don't look so surprised. Of course I am. You know that old saying, 'happy is the bride whose wedding day is sunny'?"

Mel nodded.

"Well, I'd like to add, 'And blessed is the wife who has her own money!' Lord, it sure would have prevented many a squabble if I'd had a little of my own."

"Oh?" Mel stared at her. She'd been thinking that everything would be better if she didn't have any.

"Lord, yes! Can't count the times we've raised the roof because I wanted to do something for the house and he wanted to do something for the farm. Al is sweet as pie, but stubborn as an old mule. I don't know how many times I've had to sneak or cry or raise holy smoke when he didn't want something that I did."

"But you always managed, didn't you?" Mel said, almost to herself. More to be learned from the Costello women.

"Most of the time. Most of the time." The older woman smiled as she poured herself another cup of tea. "But it sure would have been easier if I'd had some money of my own."

That's what you think was on the tip of Mel's tongue, but what she said was, "I guess nothing is easy."

"No, it isn't," her companion agreed. "Sure wasn't easy to convince Al that I had rights, too.

And with us, money was always skimpy. We usually had to choose between one thing or another, couldn't afford both.'' She smiled at Mel. ''At least you can be glad you have plenty of money and Tony's not all hopped up about it.''

Mel kept thinking about what Grandma Costello had said, all the way back to the city.

She thought about it now, sitting in the kitchen, her coffee growing cold.

She was only half right, of course. *Right* about my money. *Wrong* as hell about Tony not being hopped up.

But she had said something else more important. Men got hopped up, money or no money. Probably about a lot of other things, as well. And, if you lived with a man, you had to deal with it... ''Don't know how many times I've had to sneak, or cry, or raise holy smoke...''

Okay, I've sneaked, cried, even raised a little smoke.

Not easy.

Did I hang up on Tony because I was afraid to face his wrath?

''Hard to convince Al that I had rights, too...''

Damn it, I have the right to be what I am. I have money, and I have the right to spend it. As I please.

If Tony can't accept, can't *respect* that right...

Well, so be it! I won't sneak, maneuver, or apologize. I'm sick of this sham!

When...*if* Tony calls again, I'll tell him so.

But Tony did not call. Not any more that night, or even the next morning. She waited and waited.

That was stupid. Calling her in the middle of the night. Probably didn't want to talk to him anyway, after the way he had acted.

Over money. Stupid.

Still, he hadn't done what he wanted to do. He hadn't gone over there in the middle of the night and brought her back here where she belonged. In his arms.

She had to come back. He couldn't live without her. First thing in the morning he would tell her so. Beg on his knees if he had to.

Finally, fully clothed, he fell into a restless sleep.

First thing in the morning, his lawyer called. A representative from Tampa Florists would be in his office at nine. Tony should be there.

"Not today," Tony protested. "Couldn't they make it—"

"Today," his lawyer insisted. "Don't you know that Tampa is a chain with outlets all over the country? Not to mention their catalog sales. And I can't believe what they're offering. You be here."

So promptly at nine, he was at the office, fuming at the delay, but listening to a fantastic proposition. Fifty thousand bonus and ten percent royalty, plus fifteen thousand for signing, for exclusive marketing rights to his Melody rose.

Unbelievable. Fantastic.

It didn't mean a damn thing without Melody. Without her "Oh, Tony! That's wonderful!" Without her rejoicing with him. Loving him.

Without Mel, nothing mattered.

CHAPTER FOURTEEN

HE GOT away as soon as he could, but it was almost eleven when he reached 18 Clayborn Drive. He parked the Ford, feeling anxious. After last night's telephone rebuff, it was highly likely he would be met with, "She's not in, sir."

He thought about that.

One of his working-his-way-through-college jobs had been as a door-to-door book salesman. The very first line in the instruction pamphlet read, "After your 'Good morning, sir'—or madam—*stick your foot in the door.*" He hadn't had the nerve to do it then. But, by golly, he'd do it now! No stuff-shirted butler or whatever was going to keep him from his own wife!

He rang the bell. Waited, foot lifted.

The door swung wide.

The sight of Samuel Sands's commanding figure was unnerving. Irritating. Easy to confront, intimidate or even barge past an unknown somebody. It threw you off when it was your very unwilling father-in-law who stood before you.

"Ah, Costello. Good morning!" Samuel Sands looked less formidable in shirtsleeves, and he was smiling.

160

Tony regarded him with suspicion. "Good morning," he replied, polite but firm as he added, "I'd like to speak to my wife."

Sands stepped back. "Well, come in, come in. Join us. We're having a late brunch."

Was the man putting him on? Wasn't this a repeat of something that had happened before? he thought as he followed Sands, and found himself in a kitchen. Larger and more modern than his, but still a kitchen.

And there was Mel. His Mel. Her gorgeous hair falling about her shoulders in that familiar early morning tangle, her face, pale and lovely, above the stand-up collar of that frilly thing she had on. He was filled with a deep hunger, so overwhelming that it hurt. He stood mute, still, as if realizing for the first time how very much he loved her.

Her heart had turned over the minute she heard his voice, and she longed to run to him. But now...

He was looking at her like he'd never seen her before. Still mad! His stupid pride. If he couldn't accept a simple gift from his own wife...

She, too, had pride, rights. She had money. She had the right to share with the man she loved more than life itself. If he couldn't understand that...

No more shamming. She would not back down.

His arms had lifted automatically, but she did not, as was her custom, rush into them. She backed away, poised for battle.

"Mel..." He hesitated, baffled by the defiance

that flashed in her eyes. Eyes that had always sparkled with a different message. "I'm so glad to see you, you're wonderful." He ached to see that look again. He was frustrated. There was Sands, sitting at the table, with his coffee and his newspaper. And there was Mel, holding on to a dish towel and looking at him like she was sorry he came. "Can't we go somewhere?" he asked. "There are things we need to discuss."

"Yes," she said, not moving. "Things like respect."

"Well..." What the hell was she talking about?

"I have rights."

"Of course you do."

"And I have money."

"Oh." It came back to him then. They had quarreled about money. Money that meant so little, compared to the loss of her that he had forgotten all about it. "There are things more important than money. I realized that last night."

"Did you?" Last night when he found she had deeded the farm to him. "It's okay that I have it, just be careful how I spend it, huh?"

Damn, she was still riled about that option. He didn't blame her. He had acted like a jerk.

But now he knew that nothing mattered beside their love. He wanted to tell her, make her understand. "Mel, we need to talk."

"I don't want to talk about it. It's done." He

could like it or lump it. The farm was his. "You have to accept that. It's all over."

"The hell it is!" He was furious. Frantic! Their marriage over? Just like that! "No, Mel. I won't have it."

"That's your problem. It means nothing to me."

"You can't mean that. Listen to me." He started toward her, but found his way blocked. Sands. He had forgotten the man was there.

He stared as Sands pulled out a chair.

"Sit here. How about an omelet? Tomatoes and cheese. Mel's gotten to be a great cook."

"No. No, thank you." Why was the man talking about food when his whole life was falling apart?

"Well, at least have coffee. Sit down, Tony."

That got his attention. Tony? Had the man called him Tony? All pleasant and familiar, as if—

"Mel, honey, pour your husband a cup of coffee."

He caught it then, the amusement in his eyes. Sands was enjoying himself. At his expense! Mimicking his own words, almost to the letter, that morning at the farm, in the kitchen.

He looked at Mel. She was obediently lifting a coffeepot.

Damn it! Back under her father's thumb.

And was every important issue of his life to be settled at a kitchen table?

Before an audience that was laughing at him!

The hell with it. He slammed the chair against the table and bolted.

"Wait!" Sands called, and started after him.

"Let him go!"

"What?" He whirled around. "I thought you wanted to…to see him."

"I don't."

"Oh, for gosh sakes!" He turned quickly to follow Tony. Heard the car speed away. Too late. He looked at his daughter, exasperated. "You've been mooning for three days, and when he finally shows up, you practically throw him out."

"I have not been mooning!"

"Could have fooled me."

"And it was Tony who did the throwing. That's why he came. To throw my gift right back into my face!"

"Gift? What gift?"

"The farm."

"Oh, Mel, I don't think… Look, you had it out about the option before."

"Not the option. The farm. I bought it and had it deeded to him yesterday. I knew he'd be mad."

"Did he say so?"

"I didn't give him a chance. I hung up on him."

"He called?"

"Last night."

"Mel, maybe that wasn't why he called."

"Oh, yes it was. He hadn't called before, had

he? And today, he said he wouldn't have it. You heard him.''

''I didn't hear anything about a gift or a farm. And what's more...'' I saw him, he thought. The way he looked at Mel...I didn't see anything but pure adoration in that look, and I'm not Chairman of the Board because I'm stupid! It was almost funny, watching the two of them. He, so hungry to have her back he's ready to eat crow. And she, paranoid about his independence. Which I like. Bit too much pride, maybe, but just the kind of man to whom I'd entrust my daughter. He shook his head. ''Look, Mel, I think you two have your signals crossed.''

''You're right about that. Got 'em crossed that very first day. Did I ever tell you how we met?''

''No. I got introduced to this relationship by the media, remember?''

She nodded, a wan smile on her lips. ''And that was the beginning of the end.''

''So fill me in. How did it start?''

''It started with a lie. He was working out there.'' She pointed. ''Working with the roses. I had been watching him. You know something? I like to watch him work. He's always so intense, and yet so...well, graceful and gentle. That's funny, isn't it? He such a pigheaded macho he-man. And so gentle with flowers and with...'' She broke off, a sob in her throat.

"Okay, okay. So go on. He's working and you're watching…"

"Oh. Well, Cook was going to take him some coffee and I said I'd do it. And I did, and he thought I was the maid, and I let him think so. And that's how it started. Lying."

"Must have been more to it than a lie."

"Oh, yes." She looked at him with such a glow in her eyes that a lump rose in his throat. "It was…well, like suddenly I was free. Just me. Not shackled with a lot of money. Money can be like…well, like a smoke screen, shutting off the real you. And it affects people in different ways, I mean the way they react. Like they can't see me for the money. Men like Dirk want me because of it and Tony hates me because I have it."

"Oh, honey." He couldn't bear that wide-eyed stare that held back tears. He went over and took her in his arms. "You're wrong, honey. Tony doesn't hate you."

"He didn't…at first," she said, burying her head in his chest. "He liked me. And he was so open with me. Telling me all about his plans. He's starting this nursery, you know, and working with flowers which he loves. But he's going to be a landscape architect, and he has such great ideas. He says we're burying ourselves in concrete, and we should…" She stepped away, took a tissue from her pocket and blew her nose. "Well, things were different. He talked to me so freely and he let me help him at the farm. And he...he said he loved me. And I...oh, Dad, I'd never been so happy in my life.''

"Well, now," he said. "That sounds like a real romance.''

"That's what I thought, and that's why I kept lying. But it's not real. It's a sham." She lifted her shoulders and picked up the coffeepot. "It's over and I don't care. It's a big relief.''

"You don't mean that.''

"Oh, yes I do. I've been doing a lot of thinking, and I made a decision." She poured a cup of coffee for herself, lifted the pot toward him. "Another cup?''

He shook his head. "What decision?''

"I'm through shamming!''

"Oh?" She was shamming right now, he thought, as he watched her sip halfheartedly at her coffee, nervously crumble a piece of toast. Pretending not to care when her heart was breaking. It broke his heart to watch.

He made a decision himself. "Got a few appointments," he said. "See you later.''

"It's over. You have to accept that." Her words hit him again and again, cutting like a razor.

Their marriage over? He didn't want to believe it.

Was it her idea or her father's?

It was she who walked out, buddy. Because you acted like an ass!

Okay, okay, I did. Pure Costello instinct. All right! A stupid kind of pride, like whatever was done for my family had to be done by me! I was wrong and I was going to tell her so. But there she was, back under her father's wing, and... He was trying to hide it, but I could see he was laughing like a hyena. At me. And that burned me up!

Where am I going, anyway? he asked himself, suddenly aware that he was just driving. He had headed for the farm. Automatically, he supposed, and kept going.

If they had been alone... Why, oh, why, did Sands have to get into the act!

To protect his own, bubblehead! Just like you.

Yeah, just like me! She's mine now. Doesn't he know that I intend to protect her?

Maybe he figures he's got more coverage, buddy!

Which doesn't mean a damn thing against... Oh, hell, I love her! Doesn't that count?

His breath caught as he remembered... Mel, standing at his bedroom. "I love you. Doesn't that count?"

It does, Mel. It does. All the money in the world is a pittance against what we feel for each other. That's what I came to tell you.

It's show time, friend. You haven't been doing much of a show job. She's been doing all the compromising, acting like a scrubwoman. While you've been taking it all for granted, and bawling her out because she has a little…okay, a lot of money!

All right. Guilty. I've been a damn fool. But I'll make it up to her. I swear I will… I'll show her. And I'll show him. If only she'll give me another chance.

When he reached the farm, the debate was over, and he had gained some control of himself. There was work to be done, a plan to be made to win Mel all over again and to get Samuel Sands off his back.

He had hardly started on his pruning when he heard the car. He glanced out to see a Sands-type automobile come to a smooth stop in front of his experiment and research shop. It was Sands himself.

Now what!

Tony opened the sliding-glass door. "What can I do for you, Mr. Sands?"

"Hi, Tony. I thought we should talk."

"We did talk. This morning." If Mr. Moneyman thought he could offer a cash settlement for an easy bow-out, he had another think coming!

"No. You and Mel talked. Or didn't talk, as far as I could see." While Tony was trying to decide if that was a smirk or a smile on his lips, he added, "I'd like a turn, if you don't mind?"

I'd better head him off, Tony decided. If he tries to bribe me, I might not be able to restrain myself. "Look, Mr. Sands, I know there are plenty of money-hungry creeps after your daughter's bounty.''

"Indeed. They abound. I believe she just received a cable from Adrian Carstairs, the shipping magnate, who is eager to merge his empire with—''

"My point is I'm not one of them. You're wasting your time if you came here to bribe me.''

"I'm glad to hear that. It makes things so much easier.''

"The hell it does. Mel means more to me than money, and I'm sticking like glue. I'll sign any prenuptial agreement you want.''

"These agreements are rather tricky. I'm afraid you'll have to take her, money and all.''

"Mel will have one heck of a time getting rid of me. So you can just tell your billionaire shipping magnate to... What did you say?''

"I said you might have to take the money, too. Otherwise, it makes things awkward. Don't you see that? Now, you take your little spat this morning—''

"Which is still pretty damn funny to you, huh? Could you possibly restrain your amusement long enough to tell me what the hell you're saying?''

"I...I...'' Sands choked on his laughter, but finally managed to say, "Wait. Simmer down, son. What I'm trying to tell you is that I didn't come to sever your marriage. I came to save it.''

The statement was a magic potion, calming,

soothing. "You came to save our marriage?" Tony whispered.

"Hopefully. I thought I might act as interpreter."

"Interpreter?"

"For all that double talk that went on this morning."

"Double...?" Tony wasn't sure what exactly was going on. But Mr. Sands had come as a friend, an accomplice, and he was letting him stand out here in the hot sun while... "Come in, sir," he said, opening the door to his shop. "Take a chair. Would you like a cold drink?"

"That would be nice." Sands went in, removed his coat and placed it and himself on a bench in the crowded little shop. "Thank you," he said, as Tony handed him a cold soda from a small fridge. "What exactly are you doing in here?" he asked, glancing around at the various potted plants, pruning shears, and other paraphernalia.

"Pruning right now," Tony said. "I just signed a big contract with Tampa Florists and I've got to get these shoots ready for... Oh, never mind that. What did you mean about double talk?"

Sands took a swallow from the can, and smiled. "I mean, you were talking about one thing, and Mel was talking about another."

"I don't understand."

"You sure don't. Didn't, anyway. You came to say you were sorry, and let's make up. That kind of stuff, didn't you?"

Tony nodded.

"Well, Mel couldn't hear what you were saying. She was so sure you had come because you were mad about the farm that she couldn't even talk about anything else."

"Oh. The option. I had forgotten all about it."

"More than that, son. She's bought it, and had it deeded to you."

"She did? To me? She shouldn't have done that."

"Well, she did. And that's your problem. Just came to interpret the double talk. You can take it from there." He picked up his coat, handed the empty can to Tony. "I enjoyed the visit, son. Better leave you to your pruning. Later," he called as he went out and got into his car.

CHAPTER FIFTEEN

MEL stood at her bedroom window and watched the black Town car roll out of the garage, her father in the back, Leo at the wheel, armed with Cook's list of groceries and other errands to be dispatched. Every now and then she heard the quiet hum of the vacuum, the splash of water, or the subdued chatter of the two women who came twice a week to scrub and polish. Cook had returned and the whole place was buzzing with activity. Mrs. Cook is in charge of everything, especially the kitchen.

The house isn't empty now, Mel thought.

But I am. Empty. And lonely.

"Don't you get lonely out there at the farm, by yourself, with Tony gone so much?" Rosalie had asked.

No. Not once, she had answered. And it was true. She had been too busy. Doing everything that someone else is doing here, she thought. I'd be driving out in that old Ford with my grocery list and ads from the newspaper. I'd be scrubbing the bathroom, painting something, or making a pie.

I could do that now. I could go down to the kitchen and make a pie.

Tony wouldn't be here to eat it.

Tony. The desolate longing overwhelmed her. She didn't feel like doing anything.

Therapeutic to feel the earth on your hands. Maybe if she went into the yard to help Pete with the gardening... He was working almost in the same spot where she had first seen Tony.

She moved closer to the window to peer at him. Whatever he's doing, he's not doing it right, she decided as he snatched a shrub from the ground, and carelessly tossed it aside. Tony would never handle a plant like that. He's as gentle with his flowers as he is with... With me! She was completely unglued by the thought.

She drew a painful breath, lost in the memory. The gentleness of Tony's hands...touching, caressing, tenderly urging, promising, and finally bringing her to the peak of erotic exhilarating passion. Exciting, fulfilling, wonderful. And afterward, cradled in the loving comfort of his arms...a greater happiness than she had ever known.

Would she ever know it again?

The piercing ring of the phone cut into her thoughts. She moved listlessly to the table and picked it up. "Hello?"

"Mel?"

Tony. She held the phone close, a jumble of emotions twisting her insides.

"Mel? Mel...are you there?" She couldn't seem to find her voice.

"Wait. Don't hang up. I want to tell you something."

"What?" she managed.

"What I want to tell you, Melody mine," he said, his voice as warm and tender, as hypnotic as his hands, "is that I love you very, very much."

The words seeped into her being. She hugged the phone.

"Melody?"

"Oh. Oh, Tony!"

"Doesn't that count?"

"Yes. Oh, yes it does. But..." She came to her senses. She loved Tony with all her heart, but she would not be hypnotized into the same old sham. "Other things count, too," she said.

"I know. We'll work it out."

"You're not still mad?"

"Mad?"

That riled her. He sounded like he was puzzled. Like he'd never been mad. Like he hadn't yelled at her, called her a...a name. "I want to know if you're still mad about..." About the farm, money, my rights. "About anything," she finished.

"Oh. You want to know how I feel about that farm business?"

"Yes." Close enough.

"I see. Yes. I, too, want to talk about that. Why don't I pick you up?" He sounded like he was smiling. "We could go for a burger, or something. Get better acquainted."

Now she smiled. "All right. What time?"

"Six? No, six-thirty might be better."

"Okay."

"I'll make reservations at the Classic."

"The...Classic?" He must have been reading her mind. She had been trying to remember where to find an old pair of jeans, suitable for Beno's or the Burger Castle.

"I'll see you then, sweetheart." He sounded smug, as if he was still reading her mind.

So, he's taking me to the Classic, she thought as she replaced the phone. Just like a date. I'll wear the green dress that flares out around my knees, and the green sandals. Great for dancing. I'll wash my hair. No. I'll go to Hera's. Hair, nails, pedicure, makeup. The works. She retrieved the phone, punched out the number, made an appointment. She had the whole day to make herself beautiful. It would help pass the time until Tony. Tony! She stood up, twirled around, humming a little tune. She felt wonderful...revitalized! Ready to do a million things!

Tony put down the phone. Grinned as he thumbed through the Yellow Pages for the Classic. Show time, huh? Well, he'd show her he was ready to enter her world.

The Classic? Small potatoes, buddy...compared to her world.

Well, hell, about as close as I can get to it right

now. "But just you wait. Just you wait," he said aloud, to no one in particular.

Pretty late to make reservations for tonight, chum.

Look, I've been delivering plants there for several weeks, haven't I? Ought to have some clout, he muttered as he punched out the number.

Once again, the old Ford stopped at 18 Clayborn Drive. Tony mounted the front steps, rang the bell.

This time the door was opened by Mrs. Cook, the pleasant-faced woman who had received the empty thermos and his thanks on that first day. She seemed glad to see him. "Good evening, Mr. Costello. Mrs. Costello is expecting you. Please come this way, sir."

She led him to a room, which he supposed from the elegant and comfortable furnishings to be a kind of study or family sitting room. Samuel Sands, reclining in a big leather chair, smiled up at him. "Good evening, Tony."

"Good evening, sir." Where was Mel?

"Sit down. Sit down. I'm having a martini. Join me?"

"Thanks, but... Yes, thank you, I think I will." How could he return this warm friendliness with a refusal? He took the drink which Mr. Sands poured, and sat on the sofa. He tried to concentrate on Sands's comments about the weather and the current political situation, but all he could think about was Mel. Where the devil was she! If, as Mrs. Cook had said, she was expecting him, why wasn't—

"How do you stand on this tax situation?"

"Sir?"

"Are you for cutting or raising taxes?"

"Raising. If we're to lower the deficit..." He stopped, swallowed and stood. For the door had opened, and there was Mel. His Mel. Just as beautiful as always, but more... More polished or something. The lovely red hair, falling just so, brilliant in the reflection of lamplight. Her eyes, as blue as the dress she wore, dancing, sparkling with the message he loved.

"Hello." He could not stop looking at her. He wanted to take her in his arms, smother her with kisses. But there was her father, sitting there, smiling, as if he still found the situation very funny. "I...I think we'd better go." He glanced at his watch and put down his untouched drink. "We have a reservation."

"Yes. We'd better hurry." She bent to kiss her father. But it was Tony she wanted to kiss. Tony. Her husband. Handsome as a movie star, and looking so elegant in that dark suit and tie. "Good night, Dad. I'll see you later."

I very much doubt that, Samuel Sands thought, still smiling as they left the room.

"I better replenish my makeup," she said when they drew up to the entrance of the Classic. "And

I'd better wipe that lipstick off your chin,'' she added, dabbing at it with a tissue.

"Leave it. It's a stamp announcing that you love me, and I love you. Especially your hands,'' he added, capturing her hand and kissing it. "Soft and smooth and beautiful.''

"That's because I've had two manicures in the past three days, Mr. Costello. And that reminds me. We're supposed to talk about other things besides love that—''

"Good evening,'' the parking attendant said, as he opened the door to help her out. A moment later he was driving the battered old Ford away, and Tony was escorting her into the restaurant.

"I thought you'd like this,'' Tony said, as they were seated at a table near the dance floor. "I know you like to dance.''

"Yes,'' she said, remembering how they had danced at Tony's horticultural meeting. The only time. It had been such fun. "I do love to dance,'' she said, and, as soon as the waiter had taken their orders, they were on the dance floor.

It was so good to be in Tony's arms again, so close she could smell his aftershave, feel his heart beating against her cheek when the rhythm was slow and the vocalist crooned a love song. But she liked the fast numbers, too, liking his expertise, proud that she could follow his steps.

"You're a good dancer, Tony,'' she said.

"Right. One of the requirements when I was a gigolo."

She stopped in her tracks. "Tony Costello!"

"Kidding. Just kidding," he said, laughing.

"No, you weren't. I think there are lots of things I don't know about you, and you'd better start telling me."

"All right," he said, pulling her back into his arms and resuming the dance. "I wasn't exactly a gigolo, but…well, a kind of one." He explained that one of his working-his-way-through-college jobs was with an escort service. When a lady needed a male escort for a special function, or there was a lack of men expected at a certain function. "Not enough men for dancing partners," he explained, assuring her that it was, "All legitimate and aboveboard. No hanky-panky. Good money which I needed, and I learned a lot associating with hoi polloi," he added.

"And to think I took you on blind faith!" she exclaimed as he led her from the dance floor. "I should have been investigating you instead of worrying that you'd find out about me."

"Did that really worry you… I mean, my finding out who you were?" he asked, concern in his voice as he looked across the table.

She took a sip of wine. "In a way. But not too much. I just enjoyed being me, without money. And at first I didn't realize I was falling head over heels in love with you. By the time I did…" She looked directly at him, willing him to understand. "I was going to tell you that day, the minute you asked me to marry you. But things happened so fast and I didn't get the chance. And then...well, you found out."

"And acted like an ass. I'm sorry, Mel."

"I'm sorry, too," she said, fiddling with her salad. "It was a horrible way to find out. I didn't mean it to be that way."

"I know. I shouldn't have pulled the wronged-me act." He was silent as the waiter took away their salads and placed the entrées before them. Then he looked at her, his face sober. "Why have we never discussed this before?"

"Oh, we did. I seem to remember lots of shouting."

"Yeah, fire and anger," he said. "But not once did we ever really talk about...about anything. Not reasonably."

"Maybe we were too busy," she said, grinning as she popped a scallop into her mouth. Certainly she had been busier than she had ever been in her life.

"Or too busy loving and being loved. Don't forget that, Mel. That's what counts."

"Yes, but other things count, too." She put down her fork. She wasn't going to be loved...lulled into another sham situation. "That's what we're here to discuss. Remember?"

He nodded, as he cut into his prime rib.

"You said you wanted to talk about the farm business." Might as well get to the crucial point, she thought. Was he going to accept her money as well as her love?

"Oh, yes. That. There's something wrong with the papers."

"Something wrong? Preston didn't say anything to me about it."

"Preston? Oh. Your lawyer," Tony said. He had never seen Preston or any papers. All he knew was that her father had said she had deeded the farm to him. "He wants to see you. Something about your signature or the way the deed was drawn up."

"But he drew it up himself. It can't be wrong."

"But it is. If it's deeded to Anthony Costello. It should read Anthony and Melody Costello," he said, his eyes on his plate.

"Oh, Tony," she breathed, tears filling her eyes. "That's the way you want it?"

"Of course that's the way I want it. And I won't accept it any other way," he said. "Everything I own belongs to my wife, as well. The farm. My business. Do you know I just signed a big contract with Tampa Florists? But I wouldn't sign it until they changed the papers and made it to the two of us. Mel, things are going to be easier for us. I promise. You can get someone to help in the house and—"

But he was talking to an empty chair. Mel had gotten out of it. She came around the table and cupped his face in her hands, kissed him full on the mouth. She paid absolutely no attention as other diners gave soft cries and clapped their hands as if in congratulation.

"Oh, Tony. Tony. How sweet," she said softly, and kissed him again. "Of course. That's the way it should be. Ours. Not mine and yours. Such a beautiful solution to all our problems. You're so sweet, Tony. No wonder I love you so much." She was about to kiss him again, but he protested.

"Sit down, honey," he urged and led her back to her chair. "You've got everybody in the place looking at us."

"I don't care. Maybe I'll just get up and tell them. Tony loves Mel, and Mel loves Tony, and everything we have is ours! Isn't that wonderful? I'll just—"

"Don't you dare make a spectacle of yourself," Tony, back in his own chair, ordered. "Just eat your dinner, will you?"

"I'm not hungry anymore. But the scallops are delicious, and I don't think I've ever enjoyed a meal more. And, do you know what I'm going to do, Tony? First thing in the morning, I'm going to call Preston and have all my assets changed to joint accounts or whatever he does to make things ours. I—"

Tony gulped. "Hold on, Mel. That's not a good idea."

"It certainly is. If what's yours is mine, then what's mine is yours."

"Sweetheart, there's a hell of a lot of difference between a very small just-emerging business and thirty million dollars."

"You mean you won't accept my millions?"

"I'm trying, sweet. I'm trying." He chuckled. "Pedro said he thought I might learn to live with it. And, all right. I'll live with it. Just don't ask me to accept it. Not yet."

"We'll deal with that later," she said, her mind apparently on something else. "Promise you won't care how much I spend."

"Look, I've never stopped you from—"

"Ha! Promise!"

"I promise."

"First thing I'm going to do is take Patsy and Jerry, maybe Buddy, too, if you'll come with us, for a sail on Jake's boat. Or maybe I'll buy a boat. And I'm going to take Don to the club for tennis lessons. The pro there is really good, Tony. Just as Marie is an excellent actress. You didn't see her in *As You Like It*, but I did. Jake knows this producer and—"

"Wait a minute. You'll have to fight Pop, not me, on that one."

"Okay. Oh, Tony, we're going to do such marvelous things. But you'll have to put your greenhouses and all the business on the other end of the farm. And tear down that barn. It spoils the view.

And I think we ought to remodel the house. And you will have to hire some help. You work too hard. I hope you'll find some time to play, golf or something. And take me dancing more often, you gigolo,'' she said as she gently tweaked his nose.

She was going nonstop, and he could see no way to shut her up. He walked around to pull out her chair. "Come along, Mel. Let's go."

She stood up to face him. "I thought we could talk. Make plans."

"Show time, my sweet."

"Show time?"

As he took her hand to lead her out, he whispered in her ear, "I'm taking you home to show you how much I love you."

"Oh." She held tight to his hand, caressed it with her other one. She loved Tony's hands, too. Loved their tender touch, the exciting things they did to her.

She could hardly wait to get home, where, filled with joy under Tony's tender touch, she would bloom like a rose beneath a summer sun.

ℋarlequin ℛomance®

Invites You to A Wedding!

Whirlwind Weddings
Combines the heady
romance of a whirlwind
courtship with the
excitement of a wedding—
strong heroes, feisty
heroines and marriages
made not so much in
heaven as in a hurry!

Some people say you can't hurry love—well, starting in
August, look out for another selection of fabulous
romances that prove that sometimes you can!

THE MILLION-DOLLAR MARRIAGE by Eva Rutland—
August 1998

BRIDE BY DAY by Rebecca Winters—
September 1998

READY-MADE BRIDE by Janelle Denison—
December 1998

Who says you can't hurry love?

Available wherever Harlequin books are sold.

HARLEQUIN®
Makes any time special ™

Take 2 bestselling love stories FREE

Plus get a FREE surprise gift!

Special Limited-Time Offer

Mail to Harlequin Reader Service®

3010 Walden Avenue
P.O. Box 1867
Buffalo, N.Y. 14240-1867

YES! Please send me 2 free Harlequin Romance® novels and my free surprise gift. Then send me 6 brand-new novels every month, which I will receive months before they appear in bookstores. Bill me at the low price of $2.90 each plus 25¢ delivery and applicable sales tax if any*. That's the complete price, and a saving of over 10% off the cover prices—quite a bargain! I understand that accepting the books and gift places me under no obligation ever to buy any books. I can always return a shipment and cancel at any time. Even if I never buy another book from Harlequin, the 2 free books and the surprise gift are mine to keep forever.

116 HEN CH66

Name _____ (PLEASE PRINT) _____

Address _____ Apt. No. _____

City _____ State _____ Zip _____

This offer is limited to one order per household and not valid to present Harlequin Romance® subscribers. *Terms and prices are subject to change without notice. Sales tax applicable in N.Y.

UROM-98

©1990 Harlequin Enterprises Limited

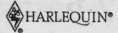

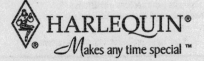

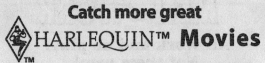 

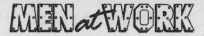

MEN at WORK

All work and no play?
Not these men!

July 1998

MACKENZIE'S LADY by Dallas Schulze

Undercover agent Mackenzie Donahue's
lazy smile and deep blue eyes were his best
weapons. But after rescuing—and kissing!—
damsel in distress Holly Reynolds, how could
he betray her by spying on her brother?

August 1998

MISS LIZ'S PASSION by Sherryl Woods

Todd Lewis could put up a building with ease,
but quailed at the sight of a classroom! Still,
Liz Gentry, his son's teacher, was no battle-ax,
and soon Todd started planning some
extracurricular activities of his own....

September 1998

A CLASSIC ENCOUNTER
by Emilie Richards

Doctor Chris Matthews was intelligent, sexy
and *very* good with his hands—which made
him all the more dangerous to single mom
Lizette St. Hilaire. So how long could she
resist Chris's special brand of TLC?

Available at your favorite retail outlet!

MEN AT WORK™

HARLEQUIN®   Silhouette®

Look us up on-line at: http://www.romance.net   PMAW2